K

In the Wee Hours of the Morning

By Anthony D Cantelmo Jr.

To my parents who were always there for me

And to my sister who made me tough

Table of Contents

IN THE WEE HOURS OF THE MORNING

In the Wee hours of the morning
The wind blows without peer
Light's are dimly lit above and
Silence knows only fear

My head was spinning from a day of frustration. In my line of work as an architect, it is not unusual for me to be overwhelmed, but this night, I couldn't sleep. I turned and looked at my nightstand and the clock read 2:34 AM. I had been trying to sleep for a couple of hours, but now I am thinking that it might be a good idea to take a walk to try and clear my head.

I got up and put on some clothes; I grabbed a coat from the closet and started out the door. As soon as I stepped outside the warm air hit me and I realized that the coat was not needed so I threw the coat on the chair next to the door and I started on my way.

The night sky was clear and there was a warm "Santa Ana" wind blowing. We don't get much weather here in Southern California, but the Santa Ana Winds are well known to all of us who live here. The Santa Ana winds are strong, extremely dry winds that originate inland and affect Southern California ... The winds are known especially for the hot dry weather usually in the fall, but not out of the ordinary for spring, This happens to be an April "Santa Ana" and a mild one at that.

As I was walking down the street, the warm wind felt like a comfortable blanket surrounding my body. I felt very relaxed and was very happy I decided to get out of bed and take a walk. I was so relaxed I had forgotten my frustration with work. It's always interesting walking through the neighborhood in the Wee Hours of the morning. No people around to break up the silence and most of the lights are out except for the street lights that glow above me.

I was about to reach the end of the street, where there is a park. As I approached the park, I could see that it was desolate. This park was a small park and you could see from one side to the other. To the left of the park was an elementary school and to the right was a wall that separated a housing tract. In the front of the park was a 4 lane road that during the day was very busy, but now there is not a car in sight. There is a library near the road and in the middle of the park was a small building that housed the restrooms for park goers to use. To the right of the small building was a small play area that had a swing set and a slide with Monkey bars for the kids to play. The park was not well lit, just a couple of lights to light up the walking path.

I crossed the small road that separated the park from my neighborhood, and was approaching the sidewalk in front of the park, when I heard laughter. I picked my head up and saw what I thought looked like a small child in the play area of the park swinging back and forth on the swings. I thought that was very unusual at this hour and I looked to see if there was anyone else around. I couldn't see anyone, so I figured they must be in the restroom. I got up on the side walk and started to walk toward the swings. I was about 100 yards away and as I got closer the laughter became louder, but I still did not see anyone other than the child on the swing. I now was close enough to see that it was a little girl, probably around 7 or 8 years old. The little girl was having a great time and was unaware that I was there. I now was about 50 yards away and I was convinced that the little girl was alone. I was not sure how to handle the situation, but I knew that I couldn't just walk away and leave this little girl alone, so I continued to get closer and as I was about 25 yards away the little girl saw me out of the corner of her eye and the laughter stopped and she jumped off the swing and started to run toward the street side of the park. I was now very concerned so I picked up my pace and followed her to see where she was going. She ran to the front of the library and I lost sight of her. I could see the road to the left of the library and now I could also see the headlights of a lone care coming fast. I was about to get to the library when I Heard the screeching of tires. I was still behind the library so I couldn't see what had just happen, but I feared that the little girl might have been crossing the street in front of the car. I sprinted to the front of the library and I saw the car driving away and I ran to the street to see if the little girl was there and I was very happy to see that she was nowhere in sight.

I crossed the road and tried to see if I could find her, but after about 15 minutes, I headed home thinking that she must have also gone home.

When I got home, I sat down and was thinking about the little girl and why she was in the park at that hour. I was concerned about her, but there was nothing I could do and the good news was that the excitement of the morning had made me very tired and I fell asleep in my lounge chair.

Sleep, a Depleted Commodity

While my head wanders
About what seemed to be a dream
The reality of the moment
Brings me back to the early morning theme

I woke up in a haze and jumped out of the chair and the first thought I had was about the little girl, but then I thought that in my exhausted state of mind, I might have dreamed the whole thing. I went into the bathroom and threw some water on my face. The sight in the mirror was a poor excuse of a 40 year old man. I looked as though I was twice my age, I guess getting just a few hours sleep took its toll. I made my way to the front door to get some fresh air and I saw the jacket thrown on the chair and at that point I realized that the events of last night were no dream.

I took a quick shower and made my way to the donut shop around the corner. I had my favorite Apple Fritter and a strong cup of coffee. Still thinking about the little girl and what she was doing in the park, I finally made my way to the office to tackle the set of plans that had kept me up the night before.

In my business, it's not unusual for the minutia of the numbers and the dimensions of the project I was working on to get overwhelming. This project was driving me crazy because of the constant changes that have been taking place for the last two weeks. I am designing a custom home for a very wealthy couple and every time they watch a home show on TV they want the latest and greatest innovations to be part of their home. The good news is that every time they make a change, I charge them more money, the bad news is that I see no end to the project and that is not good.

I checked my calendar for the day and I see that my wealthy client "Emily Cologne" was coming to the office at noon to go over the changes to the plans that she requested. Emily was a very attractive 45 year old woman, she was petite and in very good shape. Her hair was long and velvety black and her eyes were large and brown. Her 3rd generation Italian heritage explained her Mediterranean complexion. Emily was always fashionably dressed and her perfume was fresh and not overwhelming, it reminded me of being at the beach. I have to say that spending an hour or so with Emily was not a bad thing. Before Emily and her husband Lou hit it big in Manufacturing, she was a consultant with a Newport Beach marketing firm. Lou Cologne was a large man who was no stranger to hard work. He was a heavy equipment operator for years on large construction sites and eventually invented a part that made the machinery he used much safer. With Emilie's expertise in Marketing, they turned that invention into a fortune and now have a huge manufacturing company. These two people are self made and they are used to getting what they want without being pretentious.

I met Lou and Emily at a Dodger game, I struck up a conversation with Emily and after the game she invited me to have dinner with her and Lou. We talked about our businesses and when they heard that I was an architect, they told me that they were getting ready to build a home on a lot they owned in Lake Tahoe and they wanted to talk to me about designing the home for them. We met a week later and we hit it off, so they hired me, without even asking me what I charged for my service.

Emily is the one in charge of the home, Lou only cares that the garage is big enough for his 3 classic cars and an office. Most people would call this a "Man Cave", but I hate that term. I meet with Emily every week or so to go over the plans and any changes she wants me to make.

I made a few changes to the plans and I was now ready for my meeting with Emily who was usually on time. I saw her drive into the parking lot and I made my way to the door to greet her. As she got out of her black

Mercedes, She was wearing a long black dress and high heels. Her long hair was draped over her shoulders and her dark sunglasses made her look like a movie star. I opened the door and greeted her. "Hello Emily, you look very nice today!" Thank you Anthony, I have a fund raiser to go to this afternoon in Newport" "Is Lou going to join you?" She laughed, "Lou just says he will write a check and leave him alone". "I have to say Anthony; you don't look so good yourself today, rough night last night?" I had a hard time sleeping" "What was her name?" "Unfortunately, I was alone" "Too bad" "Yea" "I have the plans ready with the changes you requested". "Great, let's take a look, but I do have a few more changes for you, I know you love that". I was not surprised; we have been doing this dance for a few weeks now. After we went over the plans and we talked about the new changes she had, we had small talk for a while; I brought up the little girl in the park and asked her what she thought. She said that the little girl probably snuck away from home and just wanted to play on the swing. When she saw me, she got scared and ran back to her home. I agreed and walked Emily to her car. Before she drove off, she lowered her window. "You better make sure you get some sleep tonight and stop scarring little girls!" We both laughed and she drove off.

Emily was right, I did need to get some sleep, so I rolled up the plans locked up the office and I got in my truck and drove to "In N Out" Burger to get some lunch. I ordered through the drive through and pulled to a parking space and dropped my tailgate and sat and ate my Burger and fries. There is nothing I like better than "In N Out" although I try not to go too often anymore, but I need the comfort food today.

I finally got home and before I sat down, I turned on the TV. I remembered that the Lakers had an afternoon game against the Celtics, so I thought I would watch the game before I tried to get some sleep. I don't think I even got through the first quarter before I fell asleep.

I woke up and everything was dark, the TV was still on, but outside the sun was down, how long had I been asleep? I looked at the clock on the wall and I could not believe what I saw. The time was 2:34 AM. That was the same Time I saw last night before I decided to go for a walk. Was it just a coincidence? I tried to fight the impulse, but I just had to walk down to the park and see if the little girl was going to make an appearance. I remember what Emily said, but the time on the clock was just too much for me to ignore, so I started on my way, hoping that there was no repeat of last night.

Yesterday, all over again

When the wind blows
It brings its own unique way
One night it comforts you like a blanket you may wear
But then it may pull the blanket away
And it may leave you swirling in despair

As I walked through the neighborhood towards the park, it felt eerily familiar. The warm wind was blowing, but it did not comfort me as it did the night before. The quiet of the street made me uneasy to say the least. As I approached the end of the street my eyes fell to the ground. I was trying to avoid looking towards the play area in the park. The curiosity that dragged me here was now abandoning me and I really wanted to turn around and go back home. Why was the thought of a little girl playing in the park so frightening to me? Had I watched too many horror movies where little children are used as scary figures or was there something more to it? In my mind, I knew Emily was right, that the little girl had just snuck out of her home to play and as much as I wanted to make sure, I could not look. As I started to turn around the most frightening sound forced its way through the noise of the wind and the pounding of my heart. It was the sound of laughter, just as it was the night before. This time though, the laughter was much louder and it was piercing my ears. I now had to go to the park, I had to see the little girl and try and find out who she is and why she is at the park alone at 3:00 AM in the morning.

I made my way to the end of the block and crossed the street. As I stepped up on the side walk, I could see the swinging little girl once again having a great time. How was I going to approach her without scaring her and having a repeat of last night? Last night her laughter sounded fun and cheerful to me, but the laughter tonight was different. It seemed to be drearier and forced, but that might just be my twisted perception and me trying to make a little girl playing on a swing the next Alfred Hitchcock movie.

I slowly approached the play area and I noticed that the little girl saw that I was there. She did not stop laughing and she continued to play on the swing. I was close enough to make out her face. She was as I thought, around 7 or 8 years old. She had short blond hair, but her skin seemed pail as though she did not get out in the sun much. She was wearing a long dress, which seemed odd. The dress looked as though it would be worn for a special occasion and not to play in the park. I sat down on a bench and just watched her for a while, not wanting to scare her, but then I thought that a man sitting and staring at her at 3:00 in the morning was pretty creepy. So I decided to try and approach her.

I slowly walked towards her as she continued to swing. It did not seem as though she was frightened tonight, in fact it looked as though she was performing for me. She was swinging higher and higher and her laughter was continuous. I was a little concerned that she might fall off the swing, but she seemed in complete control. I wanted to say something, but I decided to wait and allow her to complete her performance. I figured that when she was ready, she would slow down and I could talk to her.

After a few minutes, her swinging slowed down almost to a complete stop. She looked at me and almost seemed to be waiting for me to applaud her efforts to entertain me. "That looks like fun" I said, and she just laughed. "You are really good at that, have you been swinging for a long time?" Again, just laughter, but it also seemed as though she was pleased that I was acknowledging her expertise. "My name is Anthony, what's yours" She now had stopped her swinging and looked right into my eyes and said "Jenny". Her eyes were a piercing green and it seemed as though I could see my reflection in them as if they were mirrors. "I saw you last night, but you ran away before I could talk to you" She turned her head away and started to swing again. "Is your mommy here with you?" She turned her head back and looked right at me. "Mommy is at home with my brother." "Can I walk you home now?" "I am waiting for my dog to come back; he always gets lost, but then comes back." I see no dog and I did not see one last night. Then she said something very odd "I love Christmas time, don't you? " I was not sure how to answer that, or even why she said it, but I wanted to keep the conversation going. "Yes, but Christmas was a few months ago, did you get a lot of nice gifts from Santa?" She just started to laugh, so I asked her the next question that was on my mind, "Does your Daddy know you are here?" Her voice got very sad and she said, " We were taken from Daddy" I didn't want to push that and I said, "please let me walk you home" I thought everything was fine, but then all of a sudden she jumped from the swing and again started to run towards the library.

She was surprisingly quick for such a little girl and I started to sprint after her, Again I lost sight of her as she ran in front of the Library and just as it happened the night before, a car came almost from nowhere and I could hear the screeching tires. The car sped off and the little girl was once again nowhere to be seen

I was confused, but now I know that the little girl was real and her name is Jenny. Why did she run? I crossed the street and spent about an hour looking through the neighborhood, but I could not find her and did not see a dog anywhere. I headed home and now I know that I had to find out more about Jenny and why she is playing in the park, alone in the wee hours of the morning.

Finally, we meet

Stop running Little Girl
And speak to me
Or are we destined to
The world of make believe

I got back home about 4:30 AM, but I was not tired at all, in fact I was full of energy and curiosity and the funny thing was, I was more at ease now that I actually talked to Jenny and I realized that she was not some kind of Poltergeist, but a real little girl, strange but real. I was thinking about the conversation we had and I think that she is looking for something; maybe it has to do with being taken away from her father. I noticed how sad her voice was when I asked her where her father was. I also thought that when she was performing for me on the swing, she was looking for validation, but maybe I'm just thinking too much about this and maybe it's just a little girl with an imaginary dog having fun on a swing at an odd hour.

Since I was up and had plenty of energy, I decided to do some work on Emily and Lou's plans. I rolled out the plans and opened my computer to get started. All of the work now is done on the computer, but I like to look at the large set of plans to get a real perspective of the work I am doing. I worked for a few hours and my phone rang, I looked at the ID and it was Lou. "Hello Lou, funny you should call, I have been working on your plans." Lou Laughed " I'm calling to let you know that Emily and I are going to take a trip to Tahoe in a couple of days and want to know if you can come. We need to get the landscaping plans done so we can get the approval from the Tahoe plan check." "That sounds like a good plan, Lou;

it's not easy getting through the environmental regulations they have. When do you plan on leaving?" "Friday afternoon, we will fly into Reno and drive up the mountain." "Oh, by the way Anthony, I just want you to know that Emily is Bringing Catherine." Catherine is a friend of Emily, she has been divorced for a couple of years and Lou says she is now looking for husband #2. I'm sure Emily is trying to play match maker. Catherine is actually a very nice and attractive woman. She is about 5'4" and looks as though she works out regularly so in good shape. Her hair is blond and short, but I don't think that's her natural color and she could have some Italian or Hispanic in her, so she has a nice tan. She looks to be in her early forties. I have met her once before and we had a very nice conversation. She is not looking for financial support, she has been a Pharmaceutical rep for many years, and Lou says she is just a little needy. She will be a nice buffer between me, Lou and Emily. They are very nice, but can be overwhelming at times. "No problem Lou, I will meet you at the airport, just let me know what time." "I will call you as soon as I get things scheduled." "Sounds great Lou talked to you then, bye."

This trip comes at a great time, it will get my mind off Jenny for a few days and maybe when I get back, the whole thing will be over and I will forget about it, plus Lake Tahoe is a beautiful place to go. The good news is that even though it's April, they still have snow on the mountain, so maybe I can get some skiing in. The Lake is huge, in fact, it looks like an ocean. I have been up there in summer and winter, but it doesn't matter what time of year you go, it is still beautiful and you can gamble on the Nevada side of the Mountain so that is just another plus. I now am looking forward to this working weekend.

I met Lou, Emily and Catherine at the airport at 5:00 in the afternoon, the flight was not until 6:30, so we decided to grab some dinner at a nearby restaurant. "It's nice to see you again Catherine, how have you been? "Doesn't she look great Anthony" Emily chimed in, Catherine blushed. Lou now jumped in and saved me "of course she looks great, now let's eat!" We ordered the food and had nice conversation. Emily put off being match maker at least for now. We walked back to the airport and boarded the plane, the flight was short and we landed in Reno. Reno is called "The biggest little city". Reno is a small cowboy town, known for its casino's and its proximity to ski resorts, especially Tahoe. We rented a car and drove the couple of hours up the mountain.

Lou and Emilie's property that they owned was in North Tahoe on the Nevada side of the mountain in a place called Incline village. This was a very upscale area of Lake Tahoe. This area is magnificent, with beautiful Mountain views; fantastic ski area's and beach front properties. The property that Lou and Emily own is on the Beach. Many of the beaches here are only open to people who own property.

As expected, Lou and Emily reserved rooms at the Hyatt Regency Lake Tahoe Resort. Only the best when it comes to these two people. A beautiful resort with a private beach. They reserved each of us our own lakeside cottage. Each of these cottages was like a condo. It was very comfortable and enjoyable. After we checked in, we decided to freshen up and go out to get something to eat and check out the town. Lake Tahoe is not like any other gambling area. They don't have many casinos, but the Hyatt has its own. We all met at 9:00 at Lou and Emilie's Cottage and went to the Hotel Restaurant. When we were seated, Emily looked at me and said, "Anthony, why don't you tell Lou and Catherine about your little girl in the Park". I wasn't happy she brought that up; I was trying to forget about Jenny, "I don't think anyone wants to hear about that." But I knew it was too late, as Catherine bellowed. "What about a little girl at the park?" I told the story as I had already told Emily the other day and then I added the part where I actually talked to Jenny the next night. Emily said, "WOW, you saw her again and she did not run away from you at first." I said" Yea, she seemed to be at ease with me until I asked about her father." Lou chimed in, "Stay away from that park, Anthony, It sounds like nothing but trouble. " Catherine seemed to be interested, but said nothing, so we got off that topic and decided to do some gambling. Lou and I both like to throw the dice, so we hit the Crap tables and Emily and

Catherine went their own way. We said we would meet up in an hour at the coffee shop.

Lou and I played a little craps and both lost money so we picked up our chips and met the ladies. Lou and Emily and Catherine went back to their cottages and I stayed in the casino a little longer to play. We agreed to meet at Lou and Emilie's cottage at 9:00 AM to go out to the lot and start to work on the landscaping plans.

I finished with the crap tables around 2:00 AM and headed back my cottage. I was pretty wiped out from the flight and the drive up the mountain and then the Casino play, so I took a shower and got ready for bed. My head hit the pillow, but I decided that I better call the desk and have them give me a wakeup call at around 7:30 AM I wanted a little extra time to get my supplies ready for the day's work. I hung up the phone and immediately fell asleep. I was awakened by the phone, it was still dark outside, so I knew it was not morning yet, so I looked at the clock on the nightstand and it said 2:34 AM. WOW, I could not believe it, so I answer the phone and the voice on the other end said, "This is a wakeup call." The voice was automated, so I called down to the desk and asked why they gave me a wakeup call at 2:34 AM and they said it was requested from my room phone. I told them that I had requested a 7:30 AM wake up call, not 2:34 AM. They said that yes, there is a 7:30 AM wakeup call also on the books. I hung up the phone and now was really freaked out. I did not share the part of the story about the time with anyone, so it could not be anyone playing a joke on me. As freaked out as I was, I knew I had a full day's work in a few hours so I had to try and get some rest. I finally fell asleep and got the 7:30 AM wake up call. I thought about the earlier call, but I had to focus on work.

We all met at Lou and Emilie's cottage and headed over to the lot. The lot was only a mile or so from the hotel, so we arrived at the lot and went right to work. There were many restrictions when it comes to landscaping beach front property in Tahoe, so before I came out here I got all the information I needed and shared it with Lou and Emily. We worked until 1:00 and Emily wanted to break for lunch. I didn't want to stop working, so I told everyone to go ahead without me. I knew how much work I had to do, and I was hoping to do some skiing tomorrow, before I had to head back home.

They all left for about an hour and I was able to get quite a bit done. They brought me back a sandwich and drink, so I took a break and ate. We worked until 5:00 and I had sketched everything I needed so when I got back home I could draw up the landscaping plans and submit them to the planning department next week for approval. I wanted to get the plans in as soon as possible, because I was sure that there would be some corrections that the city planners would want me to make.

Lou and Emily had no hard schedule to when they wanted to start building, but I wanted to get the plans approved as soon as possible and if they wanted changes after that, it would be much easier.

After we got back to the hotel, we agreed to meet at 8:00, so I was able to get a little more work done, and then take a shower. I met everyone at Lou and Emilie's cottage and we went to dinner. Lou said, "Anthony, It looks like we did quite a bit of work today." "Yea, but I need about 2 hours more tomorrow to get a few more elevations and then I will be able to submit the plans next week." Emily said," I thought you wanted to do some skiing tomorrow?" "I do, and I will get to the lot early in the morning and have plenty of time to ski." "Lou and I don't ski, but Catherine does" " Great" Catherine, I will call you when I get back and we can head to the lodge" " OK, that sounds great, I have not skied in a couple of years." Have you ever skied here in Tahoe?" "No" "You will be in for a treat, the snow is magnificent." Emily had to chime in, "You two can keep each other warm on the ski lift"! Catherine blushed and I just chuckled. Lou said, "While you two are skiing, Emily and I are going to play a round of golf." Since its April, The golf course is open; even though there is snow on the ski areas.

Emily asked, "Anthony, are you sure you need to fly back tomorrow night?" Emily, Lou and Catherine were going to spend a couple of more days in Tahoe, but I had to get back. I had too much work to do. "Yea, I have too much work to do." Too bad, Maybe Catherine can change your mind when you are skiing?" "Leave him alone" Lou jumped in, "He knows he can stay if he wants, but if he has to get back, stop bugging him." "Oh shut up Lou!" Emily and Lou have a great relationship, so they can talk to each other like that and then laugh. There is never any anger in their words.

We finished dinner, and we decided to head to the casino. Catherine and Emily Joined Lou and I at the crap tables. If you have never played craps, it is a very exciting and addictive game. Neither Emily nor Catherine had ever played and they really enjoyed throwing the dice. The dealers always like to have attractive women at their tables; they seem to bring an extra energy to the table. I am a firm believer that the dice do react to the energy at the table, whether it is the energy from the ladies or not.

We played for a couple of hours, Emily and Lou headed back to their cottage, Catherine stayed with me for an hour or so longer and then she decided to turn in. I walked her back to her cottage and then headed back to the casino. I was determined to stay up until after 2:34 AM even though I had to get up early the next day. I figured that if I stayed and played then the time would pass without me realizing it. I stayed in the casino until 3:30AM and headed back to the cottage. I got up at 7:00 AM, Showered and took the car to the lot. I worked for a couple of hours and finished with what I had to do. I drove back to the cottage and called Catherine and let her know that we could leave for the ski resort in about an hour. She said she would be ready.

A Day on the slopes

Tranquility and peace
The Mountain reveals
And the Silence of things
Brings perspective to even the hardiest of beings

Lou and Emily did not need the car to golf, since the course was on the hotel grounds. I picked up Catherine at her cottage and we headed to the ski area. Neither of us had our ski gear, so we needed to rent it. It took us about an hour to get our gear and be ready for the slopes. I was really looking forward to this. I had not been skiing for a while and there is nothing that makes you feel the adrenalin more than rushing down a mountain with the cold wind blowing past your face and the beautiful scenery that surrounds you.

Catherine and I got in line at the ski lift for the first run of the day. Tahoe is no beginner mountain, the slopes are long and steep. It's always funny to see people who are not very good skiers try to tackle the mountain. Most of the time they end up crashing and dragging themselves down the mountain on their but. The worst part is when a beginner tries to get on the ski lift and can't do it. They have to stop the entire lift to remove them from the lift area. I have seen some pretty funny situations, but when it is cold and the wind is blowing and they stop the lift while you are 200 feet in the air, it can be a very uncomfortable situation.

I did not know what kind of skier Catherine was, but she seemed to know what she was doing. We got on the lift and were on our way.

The one thing about riding on a ski lift, if you have never been on one, is that you have plenty of time to talk to your riding partner. Even if you have no Idea who the person is, being silent for the entire ride is hard to do. Catherine and I know very little about each other, only what we learned from Lou and Emily, but by the end of the day and several rides on the ski lift, we will know each other pretty well.

As the lift started to climb, we took in the beautiful surroundings. When you reach the height above the trees, you are amazed at the view of the lake and everything that is around it. I asked Catherine where she usually skies, and she told me that she often skied at Mammoth Mountain at least once per year, but I have not been there for a few years. Mammoth Mountain is a few hours closer to Orange County than Lake Tahoe off the 395 and is very close to Yosemite National Park. It is a beautiful place to ski especially for very serious skiers. I told her that I do mostly local skiing at Big Bear Mountain and once in a while make it up to Tahoe. I like Tahoe because of the casinos that I can go to after I ski. We talked about skiing for the rest of the ride and we are now approaching our destination. We both start to prepare to get off the lift. You want to ready yourself, because you don't want to make a mistake and fall off the chair when your skies hit the ground. It can be a very embarrassing moment. Both of us make a clean departure and we ski over to the trail map to see what area we want to ski down. The great thing about Tahoe is that it is so big that there are many different trails and many types of terrain. We decide to take a long journey for our first run, kind of a sightseeing run. It's good to take a nice long run at first to get your body warmed up and get your "Sea Legs" on your skies, especially since they are rented skies; you want to find out how the equipment feels and how it reacts in certain situations. We both test our equipment as we ski down the Mountain. Catherine is a very fluid skier, you can tell she has been skiing a long time.

We reached the bottom of the mountain after our first run and we got in line to get back on the ski lift. We both are now warmed up and ready for a full day of skiing. We sat down on the chair lift and started up the mountain again. Catherine hesitantly started to talk, "Anthony, when you were talking about the little girl at the park, I did not want to say anything at the time, but who do you really think she is." I knew that this line of questioning was inevitable since we were going to spend so much time on the ski lift, so I was ready to answer. "Well Catherine, right now, I just think, she is a lonely little girl with an imaginary dog and parents or at least one parent who has no idea she is sneaking out of the house." "But you said the second night; you really did not want to see if she was there, that you had an uneasy feeling." True, but I think that was just because of the way little children are portrayed in horror films, but since I talked to her, that feeling has gone away." "There is one odd thing that has happened that I haven't told anyone," "What's that?" Well, the first night, when I could not sleep, I looked at the clock and it read, 2:34. The next night after I had fallen asleep watching the Lakers game, I woke up and the clock read 2:34, and that is the only reason I walked to the park the second night. I had no design on going until I saw the clock and then my curiosity got the best of me." "And you don't think that's weird?" "Well there is one other thing, Friday night, I got back to the cottage at 2:00 AM and I called to the front desk to put in a wakeup call for 7:30 AM, my head had just hit the pillow and I fell asleep when the phone rang, I looked at the clock before I answered and the clock read 2:34. When I picked up the phone, a recorded voice said this was my wakeup call." "You are kidding," "No, and I called the front desk to find out why they had just given me a wakeup call and they said that it had been called in for 2:34 from my room. I told them that I had called in a wakeup call for 7:30 not 2:34, and they said that, yes; there is a 7:30 wakeup call also on the books." Catherine looked perplexed. "That is unbelievable, what do you think the 2:34 means?" "Honestly, I don't know, but last night, I made sure I did not get back to the room until after 2:34." "I don't blame you." "You still think after all that, that she still is just a normal little girl?" "I hope so!"

We reached the top and the lift brought us to our destination and we both jumped off and were getting ready for our second run down the mountain. After the conversation we had on the lift, it really got me thinking about Jenny and the time, but now I am ready to ski and I will put the other stuff in the back of my mind, at least for now.

Were ready for our second run of the day; we decided to take a more challenging run. This run was steep and had some very large moguls, which I like. The run was great and we took a few more runs after that. In the mean time, we talked about everything from how long Catherine has known Emily and Lou to her divorce. She told me about her kids, she has a son who is 18 in collage, and a daughter who is 22 and works at the same pharmaceutical company that she does. She seems to be very proud of her kids. Catherine was not real keen on talking about her marriage and I was not really interested either, but the one thing that I did learn was that Lou was wrong when he told me that Catherine was looking for husband #2. I get the impression that she is very comfortable with her life the way it is and not looking to make a change any time soon. She has known Emily since they went to high school together, and was the maid of honor at Lou and Emilie's wedding. Emily was her Matron of honor.

After our fifth run, we decided to get something to eat. It's funny, whenever you see people at a ski lodge on TV or in the movies, you see very beautiful people cuddling up to the fireplace and drinking hot chocolate, but the reality is much different. What you really see is a bunch of people looking for a place to put their skies and snow boards and taking off a lot of the clothing that they don't needed at the bottom of the mountain. It is a much disorganized place and then trying to find a place to sit and eat is another story. After about 45 minutes, Catherine and I were refreshed and ready to take on the mountain again. We were very comfortable with each other now and most of our conversation now was about skiing and different experiences we have had on ski trips. The daylight was starting to fade, and on our last run, the sunset was amazing. It's funny, but to me, skiing with the sun beating down on me is much more enjoyable then when it is snowing and today was a perfect ski day.

We finished our last run and had to return our rented ski equipment. We turned in the equipment and started back to the hotel. On the way back I told Catherine, that I have decided not to leave tonight, I am too tired to drive down the mountain. She thought that was a good Idea, so I called the Airlines and changed my flight for tomorrow at 3:00 PM that will give me time to have a good breakfast and drive back down to Reno without having to rush.

We got back to the Hotel and met up with Emily and Lou. When I told them my decision not to leave tonight, Emily chirped, "I told you Catherine would change your mind about leaving!" We all laughed and I asked them how the golf game went. Lou had told me that they both had just started to play a few months ago. "Well." Lou explained, "we only lost about 20 balls between us, and that a pretty good day if I must say so myself." Lou and Emily have a perfect attitude for golf, they just don't care. "That's great Lou, but you should have come skiing with Catherine and I, It was a great day up on the top of the mountain." Emily started to laugh, "I can't even get Lou on roller skates, let alone skis." "What time should we meet for dinner?" asked Lou. Catherine spoke up "First I am going to take a shower and get cleaned up." "OK, it's 6:30 now, why don't we meet at our cottage at 8:00?" Emily asked. We all agreed and went our separate ways.

I got back to my cottage and I also needed a shower. The skiing was great, but it sure takes a lot out of you. You use muscles that you don't normally use, I'm sure I will feel it in the morning. I met everyone at Emilie's cottage and we all headed for dinner. After dinner we headed back to the casino and played for a while. Emily and Lou headed back to their cottage around 11:00, Catherine stayed with me until about 1:00 AM and then she said she was wiped out and had to get some sleep. She knew that I was not going to go back to the cottage until after 2:34, but she didn't bring it up. I'm glad she didn't tell Lou and Emily about the time, it's too much to think about, let alone explain it to people. I walked Catherine back to her cottage and headed back to the casino until around 3:00 Am and then I headed back to my cottage.

I no sooner hit the pillow I fell asleep. I woke up around 8:00 AM, showered and headed to the front desk to make sure my rental car would be ready around noon for me to drive down to Reno. I made all the arrangements and then got a call From Catherine to see what time I wanted to meet for Breakfast. I told her anytime, and we all met at 10:00 AM at the hotel restaurant. Emily still tried to get me to stay longer, but I had to get back and thanked Emily and Lou for a great weekend and I also thanked Catherine for a fun day on the slopes. I went back to the cottage and packed everything up and met everyone back at Emilie's cottage for a final goodbye. Catherine reminded me to call her when I get a chance and I agreed. I left the cottage and drove down to Reno and then flew into Orange County Airport. I landed around 5:15 and drove home. It was a fun weekend, but I was exhausted. I was thinking before I hit the sheets, what did little Jenny have in store for me now that I was back home.

Memories from the past

Today we Wonder
What does the future hold
But stay silent on Tomorrow
It could bring moments untold

I no sooner shut my eyes, and I heard a knock on the door. I got up and looked out the window and saw that it was my neighbor Jim. I opened the door and said, "Hello Jim, what's up" He said that there was some excitement in the neighbor hood while I was gone, the house across the street that was a short term rental house had a huge party and the police had to come and break it up. The neighborhood was going to have a meeting tomorrow night to see if there is something we can do about the house and getting the owners to stop the short term rental stuff. I told him, that I would try and be there, but we really need the politicians involved. He agreed and went home. Jim and Amy have been my neighbors for about 3 years, they bought the home when the housing prices had come down and they really fixed their home up nice. I helped them draw up a room addition. Jim is a burly man who is a good guy, but can have a quick temper when provoked. He works as an Auto mechanic and works 6 days a week so he can pay the mortgage and allow Amy to be a stay at home mom for their 2 daughters. Amy is a very sweet person, she is very small, about 5'2" and very thin. Her hair is brown and very long just below her waist. She is an avid early morning jogger and also is a very good cook who likes to make pies and I am lucky enough to be the recipient of much of her cooking experimentations. They usually are very good. I understand why they would be very upset at having a short term rental property across the street, it is not good for neighborhood stability and since they have two young girls at home, safety is also an issue. I will try and get to the meeting and give my point of view. Now I just want to sleep and I hope there are no other distractions.

I had a very restful and uneventful night. I got up around 7:30, showered and got dressed. I hit the donut shop for a cup of coffee, but no Apple fritter today. I left the donut shop and headed for the office. I really wanted to put in a good day's work on Emilie and Lou's plans and get those landscaping plans submitted to the Lake Tahoe Planners. I know that it's going to take some effort to get the plans approved and I am thinking that I may need to make another trip out there in the near future.

I worked for a few hours and then my phone rang and the ID said that it was a woman that I had dated about 4 years ago, so I was intrigued at the call. "Hello Deena, How are you?" "Great and yourself?" "Very good, I was surprised when I saw your name ID, It has been a while." "Yea, I don't think we have talked since I saw you at the Pier in Huntington Beach a couple of years ago." I bet your wondering why I am calling." "I am, but I am happy that you did, it's nice to hear your voice." "Yours Too, but I'm not just calling to catch up, I am Married now, I have been for about a year and a half, and we are about to have our first child. I was hoping you could come over to the house and see if we can add a room. Right now the house is very small and we thought that this would be a good time." "Sure, when would you like me to come over?" "How about tomorrow night, you can come for dinner, I remember that you like to eat, and I think I can cook up something you will like" "That sounds great, I look forward to meeting the lucky guy you married. " "I will tell him you said that." We both laughed and she gave me her address and then hung up. We agreed to meet around 7:00 because her husband gets home at around 6:30. Deena is a nice, but very emotional lady who can be great fun, but also a real pain. She is a tall girl, around 5"8" with long legs and short blond hair. Her best features were her eyes, they were a mix of blue and green and they just could mesmerize anyone who looked into them. She got her way most of the time, because of her eyes, It was just hard to say no when you looked into them. I'm sure that's how she got her husband to marry her.

I needed a break, so I drove to a little sandwich shop a few blocks away. The shop is owned by an Italian guy, named Tony Martino. He was always fun to talk to, but sometimes he could be a bit much, especially if you just want your sandwich and get out. Today, I'm not in a real hurry, so If he takes up a little of my time, that's OK. I got out of the truck and saw Tony cleaning the outside tables. "Hello Tony, I'm glad to see you have finally found something you do well." "Where the hell have you been Pisano, I have not seen you in a while?" "I have been very busy, Tony, Some of us have to work for a living, not just hang out all day and chew the fat." "Oh, I see drawing little pictures is real work; I used to do that when I was 3 years old." "Yea, but you should have stopped using those crayons a few years ago, don't you think?" "Hey Tony, I need a good sandwich, Do you know where I can get one?" He said something under his breath and we both walked in and he made me a Tony special, with Capicola and Italian Salami, and sharp Provolone cheeses with mustard and peperoncinis. I can't get this kind of sandwich anywhere else. Tony talked and I ate, the sandwich was great and it was fun listening to Tony and his stories. After about 45 minutes, I had to go, so I paid the check and said goodbye. Tony yelled as I was leaving the store "Don't be a stranger!" I waved and drove back to the office.

I worked on the plans for a couple of hours more and then remembered the neighborhood meeting tonight, I think it was at eight at Sid Clancy's house, so I put away my work and headed home. When I got home, I saw Amy outside in her yard and I confirmed where and what time the meeting was. I had a couple of hours before I had to go, so I called Lou and went over a few questions I had. Lou, Emily and Catherine were still in Tahoe, so I did not want to take up much of his time, so I made it short and to the point. After I hung up with Lou, I set my alarm for 7:45 and sat in my chair and closed my eyes for a short nap. I was thinking that the only reason that I was going to this meeting was for Jim and Amy. I know how important it is to them and I want to give them my support, but I really would rather not go, I don't like these neighborhood get together's, I know that in the end, nothing will get accomplished, but I said I would go, so I will.

I dozed off, and then my alarm woke me, so I went to the bathroom and threw some water on my face to wake up, and I headed over to Sid's. Sid is an interesting guy; He is a widower and has a lot of time on his hands. He is 75 years old and was an accountant, so he loves the details of everything. He is actually a good guy to put in charge of something like this, because he really needs something to do. He has no family, so he is very active in the neighborhood. In some cases, that's good, but in others he just annoys people. I don't really see him much, jus t "hello", every once in a while. He lives 5 doors east of me.

I got to Sid's house and there were about 10 people there, not a great turnout, but enough so that we could toss around a few Ideas'. I told everyone that we really need to get the local politicians involved to change the ordinance and outlaw these short term rentals. Some areas have done that, but there are lawsuits pending. We talked for about an hour and left the whole thing in Sid's capable hands. I left with Jim and Amy and we walked back to our homes. As soon as I walked in the front door, my phone rang and it was Catherine. I picked up the phone, "Hello Ski bunny!" "Hey Anthony, do you miss the fresh air in Tahoe?" I do, but if I stayed much longer, I might not have been able to return, it's so beautiful up there." "I'm not bothering you am I?" Not at all, I just came from a very exciting neighborhood meeting, but I will spare you the details." 'Thanks for that, I have been to my share of those." "I just had to call and find out if you had any interesting run inns with the number 234." I find it very interesting, don't you?" "I do, but last night, I slept through the night, so I had no new encounters with little Jenny and maybe that story is over, at least I hope that she sleeps the night in her bed and stops spending her time at the park." "I hope so too." "When do you guys get back?" We are coming back tomorrow night; maybe I can take you to dinner since you treated me to such a great time on the slopes.""That sounds great!""How does Friday sound to you Anthony?" "It sounds like a good plan." "OK, Great, I will call you on Thursday and we can set up a time." "I will look forward to that." "Me too, Good night Anthony," "Good night".

I was now hungry, so I drove over to "In N Out" and picked up a couple of Doubles and fries, I love to eat my food on the tailgate of my truck, I like to watch the people as they go about whatever business they have. It can be very amusing and sometimes you will see things that you can't believe. I was also thinking about the meeting I had with Deena tomorrow night. It will be interesting to see her again and I also wonder how she looks now that she is pregnant. I was also glad to hear from Catherine tonight. I had a good time with her skiing, she seems like she will be fun to be around and also since I told her more about Jenny than anyone else, It will give me someone talk to in case anything else happens, she seems interested.

I finished my burgers and I headed home. I was ready to unwind and watch a ball game on TV. I pulled up to the house and Jim was outside, so we talked for a few minutes and then I went inside. I turned on the game and really enjoyed the time. I wanted to get an early start in the morning, so I can finish up the plans for Lou and get them sent to Tahoe.

I set my alarm for 6:00 AM and fell asleep. The alarm went off and I was up and ready to go, I had a long day ahead of me so I wanted to get going. I did treat myself to an Apple Fritter on the way to the office and I got right to work. I worked until 2:00 without a break and finished the landscaping plans. I packed them up and drove over to the Fed Ex office to send them on their way. I now had some time before I was going over to Deena's and it was such a great day, that I decided to drive out to PCH and put on some "Beach Boys" and just enjoy the drive and the beauty of the Ocean. The Ocean is amazing when you think about it, it can be so gentle and then so powerful. I'm not a guy who likes to lie on the sand at the beach; I do like to drive up and down the coast though. It is very relaxing and a great way to spend my free time.

After my Beach excursion, I headed home to shower and get ready for my meeting. I was also wondering what Deena was going to make for dinner. She knows what I like, so I was not worried about her choice in food, Although, I don't really remember her being much of a cook. I guess I will find out.

No one feels it but me

I stand here and wait
For the feeling to end
But the chill of the moment
Leaves me baffled again

I headed over to Deena's home, she lived close by, and in fact she lives in the tract across the park near my home. As I turned into the cul-de-sac where her home is, I was thinking that when I was looking for Jenny the second time, I passed buy this cul-de-sac.

I parked on the street outside her home and walked up the driveway to the front door. Deena answered and gave me a big hug. "Hello Anthony, thank you for coming." Deena was several months pregnant, so she looked different then she did the last time I saw her, but she still had those mesmerizing Blue/Green Eyes. "I look a little different then the last time you saw me, I'll bet it scares you a little seeing me pregnant!" "You look great and I have no comment on the ladder." We both laughed. "Come in and meet, Larry, my husband." We walked through the hallway and into the den. Larry got up and came over to greet me. "Hello Anthony, it is very nice to meet you, Deena has told me a lot about you." Well, thank you for having me, But I have to say something Deena, when you mentioned dinner, I was a little confused, I don't remember you being much of a cook!" "She's not," Larry laughed, we are going to BBQ." "Now that makes more sense.""OK guys, remember, I am pregnant and being ganged up on is not good for my fragile hormones." We all laughed and sat down. Larry told me that he was a supervisor at a hotel in Long Beach, in fact that's how he met Deena. He was attending a colleague's funeral and Deena was also at the funeral, because she was working for a food distributer and the colleague that died was her contact at the Hotel. They started talking and he then became her contact. They dated for a few months and decided to get married and now they are going to have a child in a couple of months. "Things are moving quickly," Larry exclaimed, and we just realized it may be a good time to increase the size of our home," Deena, stepped in and said, "Before we talk about that, I think we should eat. From what I remember, Anthony works much better on a full stomach," I Laughed and said. "You remember well!" Larry got up and started the BBQ and Deena took my hand and led me to the back yard patio. I watched Larry prepare to BBQ the steaks and Deena was getting the other items on the menu prepared. Larry and I were making small talk about his work and mine. I was telling him about Emily and Lou's Project and How I just got back from Lake Tahoe. Deena, yelled from the kitchen. "Hey, Anthony, wait until I get out there before you talk about anyone interesting in your life." I yelled back, "Take your time, Deena, Nothing interesting here." We all laughed and Deena got back to work in the kitchen. The smell of the steaks really got me hungry and Deena brought out some corn for Larry to put on the grill. They had a very nice BBQ that had a smoker attached to it. I have just recently bought a smoker so I was interested to hear if Larry has any tips. "I just bought a smoker, Larry, Have you been smoking long?" "No, I actually just bought this BBQ and have not tried out the smoker yet.""And he probably never will," Yelled Deena from the kitchen. "I will, I will, just give me time." "I guess you better hurry; because once the baby comes there will be no time." I joked. "Don't put that into his head Anthony, believe me, it was a lot of work convincing him that we should start a family!" "It's too late now, from what I see, there is no turning back," "Watch it Anthony, remember my hormones." We all laughed and now the steaks looked as though they were about ready. Deena started to bring out the other food to the patio and Larry was getting the steaks off the grill. We all sat down and ate. Deena and I got caught up on what we have been doing and Larry listened without saying much. We finished dinner and I thanked them for a very nice meal and we got everything cleaned up and sat back down to start the discussion about the home improvement.

I have a method when I first sit down with people and before I start to look around the home, I asked them what they have in mind. Everyone has their dreams about what they want, but it's my job to bring those dreams to a realistic project and a lot of it had to do with budget. The budget will be the greatest decision maker. It's funny, because I have been working with Lou and Emily and they have no budget, but that is a very unusual situation.

I started my inquiry and Deena wanted a room that was next to the guest room with a Jack and Jill restroom. A Jack and Jill restroom means that there is a restroom in-between two rooms that have access from each room. It's a way to have each room seem as though they have their own bathroom, without the added cost. Larry was OK with that, but also wondered if I thought that the entry from the front door to the rest of the home was too cluttered and should be opened up. I am a big fan of an open house, especially if we are talking about a small home like this one. You would be amazed how much moving one wall can open up a home. After I got an idea of what each of them wanted, I asked the big question. "What's your budget?" This is a tough question and many people have no idea because they have not thought about it.

Deena is a sharp girl and she knows me well enough to know that I would ask, so they were ready with a figure and from what they told me, I am pretty confident that they would be able to do what they both wanted done. It does depend on who they hire as a contractor, but I could give them a pretty close square footage price.

Rusty Old Swing

Red swing Red swing
We play on the red swing
But what once saw life through us
Now withers away in rust

It was time to take a look around and see where Deena and Larry want to push out into the yard for the extra room. We walked to the side yard and Larry turned on a light that lit up a play area that had obviously been put in many years before. The play area consisted of a sandy ground that was riddled with weeds and a slide that was for the most part a tattered display of rotted sheet metal and missing bolts and then there was an old rusty swing. The swing looked like it may have been painted red when it was new and had only 4 rusty chains hanging down where seats used to be. Deena spoke up, "I have wanted to tear this stuff out ever since we bought the house." I laughed and said, "There seems to be plenty of room here to build the new room, and it looks like this swing will just fall over if pushed." I walked over to the swing and to prove my point, I put my hand on the front rail to push it, but when I touched the rail, it was cold, as if it was made of ice. It was a mild evening with a slight breeze blowing, so there was no reason for the rail to be cold. I pushed on the rail, and it seemed as though it had grown there in place. It did not budge. I tried to remove my hand, but it seemed to be stuck there, kind of like if you licked a frozen pole with your tongue and your tongue got stuck. I could not get my hand away from the rail and then a cold wind started to blow, it was so cold that it felt as though it penetrated through me right down to by bones. The cold wind lasted for about 30 seconds I was stuck there, with no way to remove myself from the cold wind and then it just stopped and my hand fell off the rail.

Deena yelled, "I guess it's a little tougher to knock the old swing down then you thought." I realized that Deena and Larry did not sense the cold wind like I did, so I said, "Yea, It feels like it grew here."

I did not understand the cold rail and the freezing wind, so I walked back to the house and finished my inspection of the area. I did not want to let on about what I had just experienced, Hell, I didn't even know. I told them that I would make some sketches for them and see if I was on the same page as they were and I would get back to them next week. I asked them if they had a contractor, and Larry asked me if I knew any. I gave them 3 names of guys that I have worked with and with that, I thanked them for dinner and I left.

Deena walked me out to my truck and we both said how nice it was to see each other again, I got in the truck and drove back home, now wondering what was the sensation that I felt when I touched the swing. Could there have been some type of electrical current running through the old swing, but how do I explain the cold wind. I parked the truck and walked inside the house. It was 10:30 PM and I was ready to sit and relax. I turned on the TV and found an old movie to watch. I like old movies, the story line is much more thought out then the new movies.

I did not think too much about the swing, I just figured it was some electrical current that I was feeling, and the cold wind, was probably just that, a cold wind; I was thinking that ever since I met Jenny, I keep thinking that everything that happens has some weird meaning. The movie ended, and it was time to turn in. Tomorrow was Friday, and I was going to have dinner with Catherine, so I wanted to get an early start and get my work done. I set my alarm for 6:30 and went to bed.

I quickly fell asleep. The alarm rang and I woke up, but it was still dark outside, so I looked at the clock and I couldn't believe what the clock read, 2:34. Oh No! I did not want to get up, I shut the alarm off and I closed my eyes and tried to fall back to sleep. The alarm went off again and it still read 2:34. Now I was really upset, but I just knew that I had to take a walk to the park. I got my coat and headed to the door. I started my walk to the park and I was now thinking that the swing at Deena's house was some king of sign. Jenny and a swing, that can't be a coincidence. All kinds of things were going through my head, but I know that I will never get any rest until I get to the bottom of Jenny and why she is on the swing at this early hour. I of course was hoping that I would get to the park and she would not be there, but I knew she was there, I just knew it. I was approaching the end of the street, and I realized that the weather had taken a turn. When I was at Deena's it was mild, but now, clouds have moved in and it was a very cool night. I was about 30 feet from the park, and there it was, the sound I did not want to hear, Jenny's laughter. OK, here we go, but this time, I am going to get to the bottom of this no matter what I have to do. I now was determined, so I picked up my pace. Fear had turned into desperation. I now could see Jenny on the swing. Back and forth and up and down. I was several feet away and she turned towards me. She started to perform for me again. I approached the play area and said, "Hello Jenny" "Hello Anthony, I missed seeing you" "I have been away, have you been here every night?" Then she said something strange. "You know she's lonely, don't you?" "Who" "You know, the one you were with." I was very confused, was she talking about Deena, Or maybe Catherine. But how would she know and then I thought about the wakeup call I got at the Hotel, but that is crazy. "You know Jenny, I really want to take you home and meet your mommy!" "You want to meet mommy, why?" "Well, I am worried about you being here all alone and also, it seems as though you like to run in front of cars on the street." "I like to scare them; I like to hear the tires." "Jenny, that's not good. It is very dangerous." "You know when I was a little boy, my dad saw me running in the street without looking. To teach me a lesson, he made me cross the street 100 times looking both ways." Your dad was mean" "No, he was concerned about me and did not want me getting hurt and I am concerned about you." Jenny responded, "My Daddy was nice, but he is sad now." "Is he sad, because you are not with him?"I could see that she was concerned about her dad, but I did not want her to take off again, so I was very careful in my questions. "Is there anything I can do to help?" "You can bring my Daddy to me!" "I would like to talk to your daddy, what is his name?" "Daddy Silly!" "Oh, that's right" "Jenny, If you take me to meet your Mommy, I promise you that I will do my best to help your Daddy." You will try and bring him to me?" "I will do everything I can do to make that happen, but I need to talk to your Mommy, so I can find out more about your Daddy." "Can you take me to her now; I really want to meet her!" Jenny started to swing again, and then she said, "You really, really promise to help Daddy?" I really, really promise to do everything to help you and your daddy." "Do you always try to help sad people?" "If I can, if I know they are sad" "Maybe you can help her too!" Again, she is going someplace that I am not sure that I should pursue. I am now focused on getting her to take me to her Mom and I don't want to get off that subject. I really feel as though I am close. Then Jenny said, "OK. Let's go see Mommy." I wanted to make sure that Jenny did not start to run again, so I took her hand and we started to walk towards the street. Finally I am going to get to the bottom of this crazy situation. I was convinced, that if I could meet Jenny's mother, then I would put an end to this craziness.

May I meet your Mommy

I don't know where I'm going
I just know there is someplace I need to be
But the road that I am taking
Seems treacherous at best to me

Jenny and I walked past the library and were about to cross the 4 lane road. The road was desolate, not a car in sight. We looked both way's and then crossed. We started to walk into the housing tract where Deena's house was. It was a large tract and there were many streets. We turned left on one street and then left again. We then turned into a Cul-de-sac and I recognized it, I was here last night. We walked past Deena's house and through a small opening in a fence between two other houses. Once we past the opening, we entered an area that was not part of the housing tract, in fact there were no houses in sight. It was a wooded area, with old tree's, many of them were bare, tree stumps, and an area that looked like people had been using it as a land fill, old couches, TV's and other pieces of trash. We were now walking on a dirt path that was uneven. This must be an area that was not developed when they built the rest of the houses and I thought it must be a short cut to another housing tract, but in reality I have no idea where we were headed, as far as I knew; Jenny could have been fooling with me. I was thinking that I really should not be here, that I should turn and go back home and forget about all this and just do what Lou told me and stay away from the park, but I had to know. I had to know what this is all about, so I continued on. It was very dark and a touch foggy and I lost my footing on the uneven path. Jenny laughed,

"You're clumsy" "I guess I am, is your Mommy close by?" "She is just up there." And she pointed to an area past the trees. We continued to walk through this very strange area and the further we walked the darker it became. The lights from the tract that was now a good distance behind us, had faded and I could not see any lights ahead. The only thing that kept me walking is that I had to do whatever I could to solve this mystery and I was still convinced that meeting Jenny's mom is the key, although, I am getting more and more skeptical with every step that Jenny's mom is nearby. We walked a little further and I heard a dog bark. "There he is" Jenny yelled "He always comes back, I told you." "Is that your dog?" "Yea" "What is his name?" "Sinbad" "That's a nice name." I couldn't see the dog in the dark, but I could hear him. We continued down the path and to the right I could see a table, with what seemed to be a woman sitting behind it. As we got closer, I now could make out the woman. There was only a small candle that sat in front of her, but I could make out that she was a brunet, with long hair and she was wearing what looked like a green dress. I could hear a child yelling in the background. I asked Jenny "Is that you're Mommy?" "Of course that's Mommy." We were about 20 feet from the woman and she started to speak, "Jenny, Is this your friend Anthony?" "Yes Mommy". "Bring him over here so I can meet him."

This was very weird, we started to walk over, but I could not see any house, the only things I see are trees and the table that the woman is sitting behind. My heart was starting to pound hard. "Hello, I'm Anthony; it is very nice to finally meet you!" "I'm Jenny's Mom, Laura, I have heard a lot about you from Jenny." I was still a little taken back by the whole thing, It seemed so unreal, but I put my hand out and reached to shake the hand of Jenny's mom, who I now know is named Laura. "Hello Laura, I have really been looking forward to meet you, I have been concerned about Jenny being in the park at these early hours all alone." As I was talking, I could hear what I found out was Jenny's brother, somewhere nearby, but I could not see him. "Jenny is never alone, but I appreciate your concern. I know that Jenny has missed you the last few days. I then Looked into Laura's eyes and I could not make out the color, because of the lack of light, but they seemed very intense, and I said, "What do you mean, Jenny is never alone? I have never seen you or anyone else at the park with her." "I am also concerned that Jenny doesn't understand the danger of running across the street and playing with passing cars." Laura just stared at me for a few moments "Please have no fear, Jenny understands and is never alone." I did not seem to be getting anywhere with this line of questioning, so I decided to take the conversation down a different path. "You know, Laura, Jenny really seems to miss her father.""Yes. I miss him too, very much. ""May I ask what happened?" But just as I asked, Jenny came over and took my hand and said, come with me. I excused myself and walked with Jenny to the other side of a large tree, I could hear her brother and now I could see the outline of a child playing a on a swing. Jenny took me closer to the swing and it was a red framed swing with 4 chains holding the seats. It looked like the swing that was in Deena's yard, only this swing was new and not rusty. Jenny jumped on the other seat and started to swing. I started to wander around a little as my eyes were adjusting to the dark. I can now see a dog playing near the swing. I was looking for a house when I felt a hand on my shoulder, I turned around and it was Laura. "Come back to the table, Anthony." The grip she had on my shoulder was firm and it seemed as though she did not like me wandering around, even though there seemed to be nothing to see. I now could see that Laura is a tall woman, about 5'8" and her green dress was long and formal. It reminded me of the dress that Jenny was wearing. Again, this type of dress seemed out of place for the environment we were in. I followed her back to the table and as we sat down I noticed she was leaning on what appeared to be a newspaper. The paper looked old and tattered, but I could not make out what it said. Jenny yelled to her mother to come over and play, so Laura got up and walked back toward Jenny and as soon as she was out of sight, I turned the newspaper around and put it near the candle so I could read it. It's still hard to read with the limited light of the candle and the deteriorated nature of the paper. I see that the paper was an Anaheim Bulletin newspaper. I could not make out the date, but I know that paper has been out of business for many years. The only thing on the paper that I could make out is the large headline on the front cover. "TRAGITY AT CHRISTMAS PAGEANT". I couldn't read the article and Laura was walking back to the table. She noticed me reading the paper and she quickly picked it up and moved it to the seat beside her. "You know Jenny asked me to help her Father, because he is sad. She asked me to bring him to her." "Can you?" Laura excitedly replied "Laura, I don't even know who he is; I think that you are in a much better position to bring the two together then I am!" At that point, Laura started to cry and she got up and started to walk away. Before she did she picked up the paper from the seat and took it with her. It was obvious that she did not want me to read the paper. I waited for about 5 minutes and then she came back. "I'm sorry I got so emotional." "I have to say, Laura, This whole thing for the last week has me baffled. I see your daughter playing in the park alone at 3:00 in the morning on several mornings and we are sitting in the middle of what looks like a haunted forest , at a table with a candle and no other light around with no house in sight, Where the hell do you live?" Laura seemed to be oblivious to my outrage and she just calmly said, "Can you bring my Husband to Jenny?" "Jenny had a feeling about you, she has kept in touch with you, she has told you about your lonely friend and she needs you to help her." "I am sorry Laura, I want to help. But I need more from you, I need some information." "Who is your husband and where is he and why was Jenny taken away from him." "And better yet, why can't you bring him to Jenny?" My anger was beginning to reach a peak and she finally addressed it. "Anthony, I understand your confusion and I would like to help, but I am in no position to help, I wish I could be more specific, but I can't." With that, Laura got up, picked up her newspaper again and walked away and I now could not see where she went. I called to Jenny and said. "Where is your mom?" "She has gone." "Gone where?" "Home." "What home, there is nothing here." At that point Jenny said "Let's go back to the park" and she started to run. I yelled, "Wait, Jenny, Wait for me." She was running up the dirt path and through the trees. It was obvious she had done this many times, because I was stumbling my way trying to catch up to her. I was running and the fog was getting thicker and thicker. I hit a rock and lost my balance and hit the ground hard. My head slammed against a tree stump and I was dazed for a few seconds. I got up and started to run again, a bit slower and more careful now. I could not see Jenny, and I was not sure exactly where I was, but I kept going down the path. I could see a few lights starting to form ahead and I knew that I was getting closer to the housing tract that we started from. I finally made it to the gate opening that we came through and I was now in Deena's Cul-de-sac. I was scraped up from the fall and I was soaked from sweat and my heart was pounding hard, but I needed to find Jenny. I ran through the neighborhood and finally got out near the street. I saw Jenny at the side walk and I yelled to her. "Jenny, Wait" I continued to run as hard as I could, but now I see Jenny starting to run into the road and there was a car heading right at her. I got to the curb and ran into the road after her. I heard the tires skid and I picked her up to get her out of the way of the oncoming car. But just as I thought I was in the clear, my legs got taken out from under me. I threw Jenny out of my hands and I was now off the ground and Air born. I knew the car hit me and I also knew I was going to hit the ground hard. I hit the ground and started to roll, over and over. I could not stop rolling, but I could not feel anything, or hear anything. I figured I was in shock or something. I finally stopped rolling and just laid there. I was soaked from sweat and could hear my heart still pounding. I was frozen in place, then I felt someone pick up my hand and I looked up. It was Jenny. "I said, Jenny, are you OK?" "Of course silly, get up and lets go to the park" She pulled on my arm and as I looked into her green eyes, I could see my reflection. I felt no pain but my face in her eyes looked like a bloody mess. I closed my eyes in fear and just started to yell as loud as I could uncontrollably. I started to shake, I opened my eyes and I saw Laura, Jenny's mom walking towards me carrying something in her hands. I yelled over to her, "Laura, thank God you are here, Please call for help!" She looked down to me and said, "You should have helped us" and then she unfolded a white sheet and threw it over my head. I could feel my heart pounding in my chest, was this the end? I yelled "NOOOOOOOOOOOOOO!" and I took both of my hands and put them on the top of my head. I pulled the sheet off my face and opened my eyes to see. At first I could not see anyone or anything, only darkness. I rolled my body over and I seemed to roll of an edge and I hit the ground. I was very confused. I must have landed on the sheet, because I could not feel the road under me. I was starring strait up into the darkness I flung my arms in the air, trying to feel something or someone. My hands hit something hard and something cold and wet hit my face. The moisture hitting my face jolted me and I sat up and I then realized I was not in the street at all, but in my bedroom and the cold moisture on my face was a glass of water that I must have knocked off the nightstand when I flung my arms. The whole thing was a nightmare. My heart would not stop pounding and I was soaked from sweat. It was so real. The strange dream must have been brought on by the old rusty swing set I saw at Deena's.

I got up and poured a glass of cold water. I looked outside and it was a very clear night. No fog in sight. I took a shower to wash off the sweat. I did not want to go back to sleep, so I turned on the TV to pass the time. No matter how much I tried, I could not get the dream out of my head. I had a weird feeling in my stomach and I knew that there was something in that dream that must have some kind of message for me. I sat there and just kept thinking and then I remembered, The Newspaper, the head line "TRAGITY AT CHRISTMAS PAGEANT". That must have meant something. I also remembered Jenny saying she loved Christmas, and then I remembered the name of the paper, the old "Anaheim Bulletin," Maybe if I can find that head line in the paper, I can find out what this is all about.

What is in a Newspaper

I read it in the paper today
But it seemed to happen long ago
I dreamed the written word
Takes me back to memories of old

I knew now that sleep was not an option, so I calmed down a bit and opened my lap top. I had two clues, the "Tragedy at the Christmas Pageant" and the out of business "Anaheim Bulletin"

First I wanted to see what year the newspaper went under, and it looks like it was out in 1992. So whatever happened, happened before that. Then I goggled "Tragedy at Anaheim Christmas Pageant" But no luck. I then Looked up the "Anaheim Bulletin" "Tragedy at Christmas Pageant," No luck. So I searched and search. Anything that I could think of that would bring me the answer, I searched. But I had no luck and now it was time for me to get ready to go. I was having dinner with Catherine later tonight, so I wanted to get some work done before that. I showered and tried to put the whole thing behind me, at least for now.

I drove to the donut shop and I really needed that Apple Fritter today. I finished the Fritter and drank my cup of coffee and then went to get another. The girl working behind the counter, whose name is Susan, said "boy, you really sucked down that coffee fast this morning!" Susan is about 16 years old. She is very nice and very smart and is a hard worker. She is one of the few young people that you see today without some kind of piercing on her face. It's refreshing to see. She has been working here for 6 months. Her dad is a friend of the owner, so they let her work here in the morning before school so she can earn some money for her summer trip to Italy. "Yeh, I had a rough night," "Could you fill it up?" "No problem." "Thanks, Susan, have a good day." "See you tomorrow Anthony."

I made it to the office and finished some drawings that I had been working on between Emily and Lou's project. I started to make some sketches for Deena and that made me thing about the swing set in her back yard and also the swing set in the dream. I know the swing set in Deena's yard was once red, there were still some paint left between the rust and the swing in the dream was red. Did that mean anything? I finished the sketches and I know that I told Deena that I would get them to her next week, but since they were done I called her and let her know that they was ready. She told me that she would come and pick them up at 1:00, so I went to "Tony's" to get a sandwich. Tony was working the meat slicer when I got there, "Hello Pisano!" "Hey Ton I see your actually working today," "Yea, you know my wife hates to see me relax." Tony's wife Sarah is a lovely woman who works all day in the sandwich shop and teaches at the high school for adult learners 3 nights per week. She is a small brunet woman and seems to hide her nice shape behind her apron. She is tough and she keeps Tony in line, or he would do nothing but talk all day. "Tony, since your working I will talk to Sarah about lunch, at least I know she will make me a good sandwich". "You just like to stare at her" Before he could finish his thought, Sarah yelled" "Shut up stunod" "hello Anthony, What can I get for you today" "Oh. Just make me one of your special sandwiches." " Oh, by the way Sarah, no onions, I have a meeting in 45 minutes and I don't want to kill the poor gal with my breath," From behind the counter Tony yells," It's not your breath that will kill her, it that face of yours." "Shut up Tony," Sarah demands," "You have a beautiful Face, Anthony." "Thank you Sarah, You know when you ever come to your senses and leave that lug, come to see me." We all laughed and Sarah went in the back to make my sandwich. Sarah knows what I like, so I trust her to make me something good. "Are you going to eat it here? "Yea, I have some time." "Great, it will be ready in a couple." I sat at a table outside, it was a beautiful day and the sun felt good on my face. Tony came out and sat down so we could chew the fat for a few. Sarah brought out the sandwich and an Iced Tea. It was a slow day, so Sarah sat down also. We all had a good talk and the sandwich was great. She made me pastrami with mustard and peperincinies and Swiss cheese. I really enjoyed it, but it was getting late, so I had to finish and get going. We all said our goodbyes and I drove back to the office. Deena drove into the parking lot and I got up to greet her at the door. "Hello Deena" "Hi Anthony, thank you for getting the sketches done so quickly" "Well, I wanted you to take a look and see if that's what you are looking for" I rolled out the sketches and we talked about them. I also went over the approximate square footage cost including my fee and she took the sketches with her so she could show Larry. I walked her to her car and I headed back to the office.

It was now 3:30 and I called Catherine to let her know that I would be picking her up at 7:00 and then I headed home. I wanted to get a little rest, since I slept very little last night. When I drove up to my house, I noticed that Sid was talking to Amy next door. When I got out of my truck, Sid came over and told me that he had some information from the city about the short term rental situation and he wanted to get everyone together tonight to discuss it. I told him that I had plans so I would have to catch up with him another time. He left and I went inside and sat down and shut my eyes for an hour or so. I got up and showered and got dressed. It was 6:00 and time for me to leave to pick up Catherine. She lived in Newport in a condo on the Back Bay so it will take me 45 minutes to get there. It was Friday, so I knew I would hit traffic, I just hope it's not heavy.

I was driving on the 55 freeway and the traffic is mild so I made it to Newport in 30 minutes. I did not want to be ½ hour early in case Catherine was not ready yet, so I drove down PCH and listened to the Beach Boys for a while and drove back to Catherine's.

I parked out front of her condo. The Back Bay in Newport is a very nice place to live. Many of the homes have bay views and you can see all kinds of different wildlife. The area is a wildlife preserve and has beautiful wetlands. You can hike and ride your bike or kayak. It is a great place to live.

I walked up to Catherine's condo and knocked on her door. The door opened and Catherine greeted me. She looked beautiful, she was wearing a Burgundy sleeveless dress that was elegant and form fitting and light colored high heeled pumps. I did notice one thing different about her; she was now a brunet and not a blond like she was when I saw her in Tahoe. "Hello Anthony, Right on time," "Wow, Catherine, you look fantastic." "Thank you, you clean up well yourself!" I was still enjoying her look and I asked, "Has something changed?" "Oh you noticed, Yea, I wanted to get back to my natural hair color, what do you think?" "I really like it; I was always a Betty fan" "What do you mean a Betty fan?" "Well, remember the carton the "Flintstones?" "Yea" "Well Betty Rubble, Barney's wife was the Brunet and I had a crush on her." "I guess I will take that as a complement" "Absolutely" "So where are we headed to tonight?" "Well, I hope you don't mind a little drive down the coast, but I have a friend who owns a little restaurant in Capo Beach and I thought you would like it. She makes all the types of food you like" And no, don't worry, It's not a fishy smelling place, I know that's not your style" "Catherine, I love to drive down the coast, as long as you don't mind the "Beach Boy's" " Really, you are going to torture me tonight?" We both laughed.

We got to my truck and I gave Catherine a little boost up onto the seat. We started to drive down Jamboree to get to PCH going south to Capo Beach. "Capo Beach" is short for Capistrano Beach, its a little Beach community that is actually part of Dana Point and west of San Juan Capistrano. If you're not familiar with San Juan Capistrano, It's where the Swallows come back every year to Mission San Juan Capistrano. The Legend of the swallows is that they come back every year on St Joseph's day, March 19 at dawn to build their mud nests on the stone church. It is said that "St Frances" who is known as the Patron Saint of Animals, loved the birds very much. The Mission itself is the most famous of the California Missions and is said to be the largest.

The drive to Capo Beach is a great drive night or day and depending on the traffic and time of year, it could take around 20 or 30 minutes from Newport. To get to Capo Beach, you drive through Laguna Beach and Dana Point both great beach areas. Driving several miles in Southern California is not unusual, we just love to drive here and I am part of that crowd and driving the coast is as good as it gets.

I did not torture Catherine with the "Beach Boy's" we started out the conversation with the usual how is everything. "How was the rest of your trip to Tahoe with Lou and Emily?" "It was good, but I felt a little uncomfortable at times, you know, 3's a crowd," "Yea, I understand, even though you have known them for years, it can seem a little out of place." "They are really excited about the home being built and both of them really like you and trust you." "I'm happy to hear that, they are great people," "I finished and shipped out all the plans and I am hoping that they get approved quickly". "How long will it take to build the house once the plans get approved?" "Well, that all depends on who Lou and Emily decide to hire as a contractor. At this point, they have talked to a few, but have not decided on one yet." "Shouldn't they have hired one before you drew up the plans?" "Not necessarily, many times people get the plans done and then hire the contractor." "I will work closely with the contractor throughout the project until it is complete; there are always changes during the project, especially with Lou and Emily." "It sounds very exciting!" "Once the building starts, it is exciting, you will have to come and see once the building starts." "I defiantly will,"

"You know Anthony, I've been wondering," "Yea, I know and I am going to tell you all of it, but, I think we need to be sitting down, because you are not going to believe what I am going to tell you," " You are going to make me wait, Come on, Give me a little now." "No, I think it will be better if I wait, it won't be that long and I want to enjoy the drive and the company, before I get into the whole thing." "OOOK, I can wait, but now you really have me interested," "I promise, you won't be disappointed, believe me."

As we drove through the beach towns we talked about the fun we used to have as kids, being at the beach and since both of us are native Californians, we are both very familiar with the area's that we are driving through. Laguna Beach is kind of an Artsy area with some very interesting characters that hangout out there. It also has some canyons that people are always trying to protect from development. Dana Point is a small beach area with some great houses on a cliff that overlooks the ocean. When I was younger, I used to like to go to In N Out and get my food and drive to the jetty at Dana Point and sit on the rocks and eat. I have met some strange people on those rocks.

 We were getting closer to Capo Beach and I was getting hungry. I was intrigue at what kind of place we were going to. I knew that Catherine had good taste, so I wasn't concerned about the quality; I just really didn't know how much Catherine knew of my eating habits. I know we talked about food when we were on the ski lift, but it will be interesting to know how much she was listening. I am a simple eater, I like meat and potatoes and Italian food, but I never go out for Italian food, because I make my own. I also like Mexican food; I really love shredded Taco's.

I was not sure where the place was, so I was now being navigated by Catherine. She took us right into the parking lot. It looked like a nice little place right near the sand. I could see the waves crashing on the rocks against the restaurant. I like it already. We parked and I got out and opened the door for Catherine. I am old fashioned like that, I still think that men should open the door for women and if a women is offended by that, That's too bad, there are something's I won't compromise on and that one of them. Catherine didn't seem to mind and I helped her out of the truck. We walked to the door and walked in. The place was not big but looked very nice inside and all the tables had a view of the ocean and there was also a nice patio, Catherine asked me if I would like to sit in the patio and I said I would love to. Her friend came over to greet us.

"Hello Catherine, You look so nice tonight!" "Thank you Sam, this is Anthony," Sam was short for Samantha. "Hello Anthony, very nice to meet you," "It is a pleasure to meet you, your restaurant looks beautiful, I look forward to your cooking." "Sam was a woman in her late 50's or early 60's, she was dressed in black pants and a white shirt. "Where's Ted tonight?" Catherine asked "He's in the back, he will be out shortly to greet you, He would never miss an opportunity to get a hug from you Catherine, you know that." "Well, It sounds like I have some competition tonight, I said, I better be at my best." "Anthony, my husband has been squeezing Catherine for 10 years, so I don't think you have anything to worry about." We all laughed. A short man in his 60's came running from the back and gave Catherine a big hug. "Hello Honey, Look at you tonight." "Hello Ted, this is Anthony. " "Hello Anthony, I will trade you Sam for Catherine, OK." I will even throw in a free meal." Sam replied, "I would trade Ted for a free meal any day, but no one will make that deal." "You know, Anthony, We may seem a little crazy, but we have known Catherine for many years and we love her like a daughter." "I can see that and I'm sure she feels the same way about you, although she did not warn me about you, she just said that her friend owned a restaurant, but it's great to see such good friends get together."

Sam took us out to the patio and brought out some wine. Catherine was a little embarrassed about Ted, "I'm sorry about Ted." "Are you kidding me, he's great. I don't blame him for wanting a big hug." "He is a fun guy and gets excited when I come in, I met him and Sam about 10 years ago, I was making my rounds in a Doctor's office and they were in the waiting room. He asked me what I was pedaling and we started talking about certain drugs that he was taking. They asked me to join them for lunch and the rest is history." "Really Catherine, they seem like great people, I like people like that, they really seem to care about you and that makes you very lucky," "Thank you for understanding" I don't think Catherine was really embarrassed, I just think she was concerned that I might be uncomfortable, but I wasn't . It takes a lot to make me uncomfortable and this actually made me feel comfortable, they were real nice people.

Sam brought us out some stuffed mushrooms for appetizers and then handed us the menus, but I already knew what I was going to order. I waited for Catherine to decide and we were ready, so, Catherine ordered Honey Roasted chicken with salad and veggies. "Sam, I saw that chalkboard menu as we came in, so I will have the 16oz Prime Rib end cut if possible, with house fries and Au Jus and straight Horse Radish. Also, could you bring me an Iced Tea?" Sam said, Wow, you really know what you want don't you" "I love Prime Rib and as soon as I saw it on the menu, my mouth started to water." We all laughed. Sam Left and I could feel Catherine wanting to hear about what has gone on with me and the little girl in the park, but I was going to stay silent until she could not take it anymore. "It looks like you picked a perfect place to eat." "Don't try and make small talk, come on, give it up." "What are you talking about?" As I smiled like I was confused. "Come on, Come on, I can't wait any longer tell me." "Ok, I will, but you have to promise not to think that I have gone crazy, because this story is getting weirder and weirder," "I promise, now tell." "Well, it all started when I got a call from a women that I knew about 4 years ago and had not seen or talked to in 2 years. Her name was Deena and she was going to have a baby and her and her husband wanted to talk to me about building an extra room. I went over her house and we had a nice dinner. We talked about the remodel and then I started to do my inspection of the property. The extra room was going to be in the area off a side yard, so Larry, who was Deena's Husband, turned on a light, so I could see the yard. In the yard was a play area that was very old and deteriorated. There was a swing in the area that was very old and very rusty, but there was some red paint patches, so it seems as though the original color of the swing was red. So far, so good." As I was telling the story, Catherine was intently listening with all of her attention. "I said to

Deena and Larry, it looked like the swing would just fall over if it was pushed and I went to the swing to prove my point. I stepped in the play area and put my hand on the front rail of the swing and it was Ice cold. There was no reason for that because the night was mild and just a slight wind was blowing." Catherine jumped in with a question, "What do you mean ice cold?" Well. It felt like the pole was frozen, but there was no Ice on the pole" "That's really weird" "Yes, but it gets better, I pushed the rail to see if It would fall over, and it felt like it grew there, it did not budge and then I could not get my hand off the rail. It was as if the rail had just grabbed my hand and would not let go. The only way I could describe it, is if you were to lick a frozen pole and your tongue got stuck to it. That's how it felt." "Is there any way to explain that?" " The only thing I could think of was that maybe there was some kind of electrical current running through the pole, But that doesn't explain the cold," But that was not all, as I was stuck to the rail, a very cold wind started to blow and it was so cold it seemed to penetrate right to my bones." "The wind seemed to last for about 30 seconds and then abruptly stopped and when it did, my hand fell off the rail." "You have to be kidding?" "The other strange thing was that neither Deena nor Larry notice anything, because the only thing Deena said was "It seems as though the swing is going to be harder to knock down then you thought." So it was obvious to me that I was the only one that felt whatever had happened. At this point I just wanted to leave, so I finished with my inspection and told them that I would make some sketches and get back to them. "You must have been freaked out?" "I think more confused than anything, and then I thought that because of the Little Jenny thing that I might be thinking that everything that happens is some kind of weird phenomenon. "Well. You were right, that was weird." "That's not all that happened," "What else?" I then I told Catherine about the dream and the look on her face was of amazement.

After I told her about the dream, I wanted to ask her something that I was uncomfortable asking, but I needed to ask. "Catherine, I am going to ask you something and if you think it's too personal, Please feel free not to answer and I will understand completely. "No problem, Anthony, You can ask me anything." Ok, in the dream, I left something out that Jenny said and her mother also mentioned." "What is it?" "Well when I first walked up to Jenny in the dream, She said she had not seen me in a few days, and I told her I was away and she said, and this is the part that I want to ask you about. Now it's only a dream and probably does not mean anything, but Jenny said" "She's lonely." I asked her who, and then she said, "The one you were with." "So my question is, Catherine, are you lonely?" "That is strange, Anthony, but my life has changed dramatically in the last couple of years and I went from a full house to an empty house, so to answer your question, sometimes I'm lonely." "That makes perfect sense and I'm sorry I asked, but I'm trying to make sense of this whole thing." "No problem, but do I give off the impression that I am lonely?" "No, other than the dream, it never entered my mind, but maybe that shows I'm a little insensitive." "I really am glad you didn't think I was lonely, because that's not the impression I want to make." "Well you don't give any indication that you are lonely, but I'm sorry at times you are" "It's just life, there always going to be something." "Yea, I guess you are right." We both fell silent for a few moments to let that uncomfortable moment pass and just then, perfect timing the food arrived. I smelled the Prime Rib and commented, "Sam the food smells great!" Catherine jumped in, "You know Anthony, the one thing I am finding out about you, is that you love to eat." "That is a very true statement and when I get food like this, it is very exciting." We both started to eat and Catherine asked," What do you think happens now, after the dream?" Well, I have a couple of things to think about in the dream, first the Name of the paper, The "Anaheim Bulletin". Since it has been out of business for years, I think it is interesting that it would even come up in a dream and the headline of the front page, "Tragedy at Christmas Pageant". Those two things I think have meaning. I tried to search this morning, but I had no luck." "You know Anthony, I search thing all the time for my work, and if you don't mind, I would like to help you with this." "I don't mind, but I hate to take up your time, I know you work hard and your free time is important." "Don't worry; it will just help me not be lonely!" She laughed and I think that comment of hers really put that uncomfortable moment behind us.

"Ok, how about this. I will pick you up tomorrow and we can get some lunch and then come to the house and search. I could even take you to the park where all this is happening." "I would love to see the park, the center of the mystery." "Great, how does 11:00 AM sound?" "Very good" "Well, maybe with the both of us working on it, we can get to the bottom of this, if there is anything to get to the bottom of." "I think that at the least, it will be fun to work on it and maybe even solve the mystery," "You know, Anthony, the one thing that we might be overlooking in all this is the 2:34 time. I get the feeling, that there may be a meaning to that." "You might be right."

We ate our dinner and it seemed as though Catherine was looking forward to working on the mystery. I was glad she was willing to help. Most people would just think I was insane, that includes me.

Sam came back and asked how we liked the meal. I said, "Everything was wonderful" "Would you like some desert." "I looked at Catherine and she declined, so I did too. "Well, Ted had to go, but he wanted you to know that the dinner was on him tonight, he was so glad to see you Catherine, that he said to enjoy and he was sorry he had to leave. "Well, I guess he deserves an extra hug the next time I see him, give him a big kiss for me Catherine exclaimed!" "Me too" I joked and with that Catherine and I left.

We got to the truck and I helped Catherine in and then entered the driver's side. When I got in, Catherine said," If you have a sweet tooth, There is a very good Ice Cream shop near the Jetty in Dana Point?" "Catherine, I always have a sweet tooth, lets head over." We got to the Ice Cream shop and Catherine had a vanilla cone and I ordered a Chocolate Chip and Coffee Cone. Once we got our ice cream we walked over to the jetty to enjoy the desert. The Jetty was much different than it used to be. There were buildings now that were not there before, but it was still a nice place to sit on the rocks and just enjoy the ocean. As we sat there eating our ice cream, Catherine said, "Anthony, call it woman's intuition, but I think our search is going to find something, I don't know what, but there is something to this mystery, I know it." "Well, I would never doubt woman's intuition, and before the dream, I really thought that this was all a creation of my imagination. Yes, Jenny was real, but the mystery was something that I doubted." "But what about your friends house and the swing set, that had to have some effect on you," Catherine said forcefully. "But that night when I got home, I was trying to rationalize that until I fell asleep and then everything changed." "Ok. Let me ask you this, let's say we find something, have you thought about what you will do then?" "I don't know, but I think the key now is Jenny's father. At first I thought that Jenny's mother was the key, but now I think it's her father. If we find something and it leads us to her father, then I will have some decisions to make." "I don't envy you if that happens." Then I jumped in with a final thought." You know Catherine, the reality is, we may find nothing and this hopefully will pass and I will be able to sleep before 2:34 AM.

We finished our Ice cream and walked along the rocks for a while and then we started back to Newport to take Catherine home. We got to Catherine's place and I walked her to her door. She gave me a big hug and I thanked her for a great night and told her that I would pick her up at 11:00 AM tomorrow and with that I left for home.

I got home and turned on a Clipper game that I had recorded. After the game I turned in.

Visiting the place it all began

Her curiosity is compelling
Her skepticism is clear
I wait to see her face
When the spirit of the night appears

I got up at 7:00 AM and did some cleaning before I picked up Catherine. I knew she would enjoy going to the park to see the origination of the mystery. She seems to be enjoying the thought of discovering something, but I really hope we don't find out anything and that way I can forget about this whole thing and chalk it all up to coincidence, imagination and a bad dream. The practical side of me thinks that what will happen, but I do have a strange feeling that there may be something more to it.

I went to the store and bought some stuff to make pizza. I thought that it would be nice to have something home made later rather than go out again. I prepared everything and then it was time to head out to get Catherine. I really enjoy spending time with her, she is fun to be around and I get no impression that she is looking for anything long term from me. I do, in the back of my mind have some worry about her being Emily and Lou's good friend, these things sometimes have a way of turning south and then everyone gets upset, so I want to be careful.

I got to Catherine's place and we stopped to get some lunch and headed back to start the search. When we got to my place, the first thing we did was take a walk to the park. "Here is the path Catherine that I take to the park, are you excited to see the haunted play area?" "Very excited, In fact a little nervous." "I think you can be relaxed, I don't think that Jenny will make an appearance during the day, she seems to be nocturnal, kind of like me." "You know, Anthony that is one thing I wanted to ask you. In Tahoe and here, you don't seem to sleep much, is that your normal pattern or is this new thing due to the circumstances?" "No, the circumstances have nothing to do with it, I really don't sleep much. Maybe 3 or 4 hours a night." " I don't know how you do that, I would not be able to stand up if I don't get at least 6 or 7 hours and I like to get more if I can" "Well Catherine, I guess I'm weird." "I think you might be." We both laughed and then I said, "After this episode is over, you may think that I'm more than weird." "We will see." "Yes we will." "I hope Catherine that no matter what happens; we can hit the slopes one more time before the snow melts." "Yes, we have to do that."

We got to the play area and it was empty, no Jenny. I think that Catherine was hoping to see something. Catherine got on the swing and I said, "Do you feel any vibrations?" "Maybe." We both laughed and headed home. We both pulled out our laptops and started to search. Catherine was pounding away at the keys on her laptop, she was intent on finding something. "Can I get you something to drink, Catherine?" "Water will be good, thank you." I got her a bottle of water and she continued to search. After a couple of hours. She screamed, "I DON'T BELIEVE IT!" "What did you find Catherine?" You are not going to believe this, but you are not crazy," "Let me see" "I went over to her laptop and there it was, an old "Anaheim Bulletin" Headline "Tragedy at Christmas Pageant" "Oh my God, there is the paper I saw in my dream, what year is that?" "You're not going to believe it Anthony, but it's 1972." "Catherine, that's 45 years ago. I don't believe it." "What does the article say?" "Anthony, you better sit down for this." The article says that there was a Christmas Pageant and after it was over, 3 people were killed by a drunk driver. The people who were killed were a mother and 2 children, while the father was looking on." "Let me take a look" "the accident happened at the school next to the park while they were crossing the 4 lane street in front." "This is crazy." It mentions the father's name, but not the mother or the children." "The father's name is "Walter Crane" of Anaheim."

"Anthony, what are you going to do now?" "Catherine, I know what I have to do, but it is not going to be easy." "What's that?" "I need to find "Walter Crane" and talk to him." "If you do find him, what would you say to him?" "That is a real good question, I really don't know, but the one thing I do know is that everything that has happened is not an accident or coincidence. Jenny wanted me to find this information and until I help her, I am not going to be able to get this out of my mind." "What do you think helping her means?" "Somehow, Catherine, she wants her father to be brought to her, and what that means is beyond me." "Anthony, I'm sorry that I found this information, before, this was just a mystery, but now, I don't know what it is, but I don't have a good feeling about it." "Catherine, Please, don't worry, it had to be found and you did me a favor. Now, I know what has to be done, I just don't look forward to doing it." "What if you just ignore it and let time pass and not do anything, I'm telling you Anthony, I don't like this whole thing and I really think you need to ignore this and just stay away from the park. These are things that really should not be messed with." I now want to change the subject, because I sense that Catherine is feeling responsible for this." "Catherine, you know what I think?" "What?" "I think we should eat the pizza I made." "Really, you want to eat after all we found out, cant anything get in the way of your appetite." We both laughed. "No, and I want you to forget about this." "Ok, let's eat your pizza."

We ate the pizza and we talked about what we found and I said, "Catherine, I want you to forget about this now, I know you feel uncomfortable, but I don't want you to worry, Everything is going to be OK," " Are you sure about that?" "I am absolutely sure." "Does this mean you don't want me to search for any more information?" "Yes. I don't want you do anymore on this. I can see in your face, its bothering you and I don't want that." "Ok, but I still am worried about you, can you at least keep me informed about what you do or what you find out, I promise I won't let it bother me." "I will," Just then my phone rang and it was Deena. I let it go to voice mail. My voice mail converts to text so I can read it. It said that they liked the sketches. Catherine asked, "What are you reading?" "My voice mail turns into text and that way I can read it. The funny thing is that sometimes it doesn't understand a word and it puts some other word in its place, it can be pretty funny." "See, this is from Deena and it says they like the sketches I drew." "That's great, I need to get that on my phone" "Yea, I really like it."

The phone call broke up the conversation about the whole Jenny thing and that was a good thing. It was time to take Catherine home. The drive to Newport was a little quiet. When we got there, I parked and I walked Catherine to her door. She put me in a big bear hug and said, is there any way I can stop you from doing anything more on this mystery?" "Catherine, I just don't want you to worry, like I said, everything is going to be fine." With that, I started to walk away and she just called my name, "Anthony" "Yes Catherine," "Nothing" "Good Night Catherine".

As I drove home, I was thinking how I was going to find Jenny's father and is he even still alive. 45 years is a long time, he would be at least in his 70's. I got home and was worn out by this whole thing. I was actually relieved that we found the information. Yes, it's weird, but at least I know I'm not crazy. Let's say that the whole thing is true and Jenny was trying to get a message to me. Well I got the message, so maybe now I will not be having any more bad dreams.

Time to get things going

You work to complete a dream
You strive for the far reaching goal
And when reality seems to be near
You can't wait to make the dream whole

April was in its last day and tomorrow, Monday is May 1st and I was
hoping that I would hear something from the Lake Tahoe Planners about
the approval of the plans, or if there is something else that needs to be
done. Today, I'm just going to hang out and try and relax. It has been a
very active couple of weeks and getting some relaxation will be good. I
am going to put the whole Jenny thing out of my mind for today and
tomorrow I will think of the next step I will take.

Now we are right in the middle of spring and the year is flying by. It was
7:00 AM on a Monday and time to get back into the groove of work. I got
cleaned up and headed to the Donut shop, but no Apple Fritter today, just
coffee. "Hello Susan, just Coffee today" "Ok Anthony, I will have It for you
in a minute." "How are you doing saving for you Italy trip, are you on
track." "Yea, but you could give me a nice tip to help me along." "Ok, Ok, I
get the message, but really, you will love Italy, there is so much to see." "I
am really looking forward to it and the family that I am staying with is real
nice and they have a daughter my age so she is going to be my guide."
"That sounds great, but just one bit of advice, don't take too much
luggage, you will not need it and it will be a real hassle to lug around,
believe me, I am talking from experience." "Thanks for the advice." Susan
handed me my coffee and I handed her a $20 and I said "keep the
change!" "Wow, thank you Anthony I really appreciate it," "I know you
do, see you tomorrow Susan." "Bye Anthony."

I headed to the office and then just when I got inside my phone rang and it was the city of Tahoe, letting me know that there are just a few changes I need to make to the plans but I need to make them at the desk in Tahoe, because the planner has a few questions and has to see me in person. I guess I am going to Tahoe.

I dialed Lou's number. "Hello Lou," "What's up Anthony?" "Well, I just got a call from Tahoe planners and they need me to make a few desk changes, but I have to do it in person, so I need to go back." "When do you want to leave, I will have my secretary make the arrangements?" "Tomorrow will work and that way I hope to have everything wrapped up by Wednesday." "Wow that sounds fantastic, I will let Emily know." "I will have my secretary "Deirdre call you with the arrangements." "Great Lou, I appreciate that." "Anthony, do you need anything else from me?" "I don't think so, I think its good news that they want some desk changes, so I don't anticipate any problems, if I run into any, I will call you." "Ok, just keep in touch."

As soon as I hung up the phone, it rang again and it was Deena. "Hello Deena." "Hi Anthony, Larry talked to a couple of the contractors and he has a few questions, do you have any time tomorrow?" "I will be going out of town for a few days, is there any way he can come to my office this morning, I will be here for a few hours?" "Let me ask him, one sec." "Anthony, He said he can be there in an hour." "Great, I will be here." "Thanks Anthony." "No problem, goodbye Deena," "Goodbye."

I am very happy that it looks like I am going to get the Tahoe plans wrapped up, at least for now. I know Emily will want changes as the building goes on, but getting the approval is the most difficult part, making changes here and there will not be a problem that is normal. I see Larry driving into the parking lot and then he walked into the door. "Hello Larry." "Hello Anthony thanks for seeing me on such short notice, but I had a few questions and like I told you, with the baby coming soon, everything seems to be moving so fast." "No problem, how can I help you?" We went over some things that he talked to the contractors about and I gave him my opinion, we talked for about 45 minutes and he seemed to be satisfied. "Larry, If you have any other questions, or want me to talk to the contractors, please don't be afraid to let me know, I will be happy to help." "Thank you so much, this is very much out of my comfort zone." "Larry, let me give you just a little advice, even though things seem to be moving quickly for you, when it comes to this project, slow down. You don't want to be rushed, you want to do it right and remember the baby will not know if you are running a little late." "Thanks Anthony, that helps a lot." "Have a good day Larry." "You too." Larry left and I finished up a couple of other things when Deirdre called and game me all the flight and room information. Of course Lou had her put me up in the cottage; those people really take care of things first class.

I headed to the store to pick up a few things for my trip and I headed home. I thought I should call Catherine to see how she was doing, I know that yesterday was a strange day for her and when I left she seemed to be uncomfortable. I wish she did not get involved with the whole thing. I dialed her number and she answered, "Hello Anthony." "Hello Catherine, How are you today." "I'm Ok." "Well I want to let you know that you don't have to worry about anything, I need to go back to Tahoe for a few days to get the plans wrapped up, so I won't have any time for other things." "I am glad to hear that, but jealous, are you going to do any skiing?" "No, this is all business, I am hoping to get the plans approved and once I do that I will be coming back." "Too bad, seeing that beautiful snow and not being able to play in it." "Ok, don't be cruel." "When are you leaving?" My flight is at 10:00 Am tomorrow." "Are you leaving from Orange County?" "Yea." "Why don't you let me take you to breakfast before you leave?" "You know I can't turn down food. Where do you want to meet?" "There's a nice little coffee shop on Jamboree not too far from the Airport." Ok, how does 8:00 AM sound?" "I will see you then." "Goodbye Catherine." After I got off the phone, I packed my bags and loaded everything in the truck so I would not have to think about it in the morning. I figured if I left at 7:15 AM, I should be on time for Breakfast.

I made a few other business calls and sent out a few e-mails and then turned on the TV to see if there was a game on. Watching sports relaxes me, so I try to find a game when I can. I like to record the games and watch them at night, that way I can enjoy them without other distractions. I found one, Cleveland and San Antonio. Should be a good game.

My alarm went off a 6:00 AM, and I got up and hit the shower. I headed to Newport to meet Catherine. The traffic was pretty heavy on the 55, but I had plenty of time. As most people know, driving in Southern California means driving in traffic. There are few times that you can travel the freeways without sitting in bumper to bumper traffic, maybe at 3:00 AM, but that's not a guarantee. I drove into the driveway of the coffee shop at 7:55 and I see Catherine's car, so I went inside. I saw Catherine and I walked over and sat down. "Good Morning Catherine, thank you for getting up early to send me off with a good breakfast." "My pleasure how was the drive?" "Busy, but it flowed Ok." The waitress came over and I said, I am ready to order, How about you Catherine?" So Catherine ordered and then she said, "Do you ever look at menu's, How did you know what this place had, have you been here before?" "No, I haven't been here, but places like this, always make good omelets, and I like a Denver omelet with extra cheese inside, so I don't need a menu." "You didn't need one the other night either." "No, but Sam had a written menu at the door, so I knew they had prime rib. You see Catherine, I'm a trained observer. In my business, I have to observe people and listen at the same time, because their words only tell me part of the story, their body language tells me the rest." "I don't know if I should be impressed or scared." "Maybe you should be both." We both laughed and the waitress brought me an Iced Tea and Catherine her Coffee. I asked Catherine if she had a busy day planned and she said she had 5 stops so it is a light day. "Are you excited about your trip; I know how much you like Tahoe." "I'm not excited about the trip, but I am happy at the thought of getting the plans approved for Lou and Emily." "Are you surprised that they asked you to come in person." "No, it happens all the time, it's just unusual for me to have to travel a long way to make a few changes, but I think its good news that they want me there in person. If it was a lot of changes, they would have just sent them back to me with a bunch of red all over them." "How long do you think it will take you to finish?" "I hope to get back maybe Wednesday night at the latest Thursday; it's going to be a lonely trip." "Oh, I'm sure you will find some way to amuse yourself, like maybe the Crap tables." "Well, I have to do something." At that point the food came and we ate and then it was time for me to head over to the Airport, so I walked Catherine to her car and thanked her for meeting me this morning. She wished me a good trip and we both went on our way.

The flight was short and I landed in Reno and got my rental car and drove up the mountain. I checked in the cottage and it was too late to go to the planning department, so I went to the hotel coffee shop and got something to eat. I walked around town for a while then headed to the casino and the crap tables. I played for a couple of hours and then back to the cottage. I wanted to get to the planners as early as possible so the earliest would be 9 AM. So I called in a wakeup call for 7:30 AM and went to bed.

Fragrant dreams

A fragrance can spark the mind
To memories lost long ago
But will the smell that seemed so innocent
Bring us nightmares from times of old

I was awakened by a loud knocking on the door. I got up and went to the door. I looked out the window and I did not see anyone. I thought it might have been someone who had too much to drink and forgot where there room was, so I turned to go back to bed, when I noticed the clock on the desk. It read, 2:34 AM. I was hoping at least for now, that I was past that, but for some reason, the knock on the door at this hour was telling me something. I put on some clothes and put on my jacket and opened the door. There was no one there, but I noticed some activity across the grass area. I closed the door behind me and started to walk to the other side of the grass and I noticed some people having a little party, so I headed back to the cottage. I opened the door and I walked over to the table to put down my keys and I saw a bottle of "Brut by Faberge" Cologne sitting there. That was not there before I walked outside. I picked up the bottle and it was opened and used. I now wondered if there was someone in the cottage, so I walked around to check, but the place was empty. Was this another message from Jenny, maybe she is getting impatient and just wants to remind me to help her? The 2:34 on the clock and the cologne on the table again are strange. I guess, when I get back I am going to have to start to search for her father. I have decided not to tell Catherine anything right now. She seemed really freaked out and when she found out I was going out of town I think she was relieved and hoped that I would be too busy and this all would go away. It's obviously not going to go away.

I sat in the chair and turned on the TV. I found a movie to watch and I fell asleep. The wakeup call came in at 7:30 and I got up from bed, but I don't remember getting back in bed and the TV was off. Did I turn it off? I went over to the table to see the cologne and it was gone. No cologne. I'll bet it was a dream again. It seems as though this is the way Jenny is communicating with me, she is invading my dreams to get her point across. I'll be her father used that cologne. It makes sense that she would use cologne since the sense of smell is one of the best ways we remember and I'll bet to a little girl, her father's cologne made a strong impression on her.

I had to put this out of my mind, I had work to do. I drove over to the city and spoke to the planner. I made the changes that they wanted and got the stamp of approval. I went outside and called Lou. "Hello Lou." "How's it going up there Anthony?" "Great, I made the changes and the plans are approved." "That's terrific, what do we do next." "Do you want me to pull the permits, or do you want to wait until you hire the contractor?" "Go ahead and pull the permits and when you get back, come over the house and we will talk." "Ok, I will get it done and I guess I will be back tomorrow afternoon." "No problem, whatever time you get back, we will wait for you" "Emily is going to be so excited." "Ok Lou, I will get this buttoned up." "Great job Anthony, I will see you tomorrow."

I headed back inside and pulled the permits to build. I rolled up the approved plans and headed back to the hotel. I went to the restaurant and had some lunch. I was feeling pretty good about getting the plans approve, but I was surprised that Lou wanted me to meet them at the house when I get back. Maybe they just wanted to look at the approved plans, but I guess I will find out what they want when I get there.

Searching for the answers

Looking for the answers
Seems like a good idea at first
But answers when discovered
May bring tragedy unearthed

I hung out in the cottage and then spent a few hours in the casino. My flight was at noon tomorrow, so I will leave here at 9 AM and head to Reno to catch my flight. I had an eventless night which was a good thing, no dreams of cologne or anything else. I woke up at 7 AM and got some breakfast and drove to Reno.

I landed in Orange County at 2:30 PM and drove over to Lou and Emilie's. They were excited to see me and we talked about the plans. I asked them if they had decided on a contractor and they said that they wanted to talk to me about that. "Anthony, Emily and I have been talking and we want you to run the job for us." "You want me to act as the contractor, Lou." "Yes, we trust you and think you will do a great job." "I appreciate that, but you know that I have never done that before and I'm not sure you want me to have on the job training for your home." "Anthony, we know you can do it and we are willing to give you the support you need." We talked about the logistic problem and many other issues that will arise from this arrangement if I decide to do it. "We have already rented the cottage that you stayed in for one year for you to use anytime you have to go to Tahoe and we have arranged an expense account for you." "Well Lou and Emily, it looks like you have thought this through, so I accept. I do need about 3 weeks to finish up some projects I'm on and then I will put my full attention to your home." "That sounds great, we are very excited you are going to be in charge and we know you will do a great job, now

let's get some dinner, to celebrate, what do you say?" That sounds great."
"Emily jumped in, I'm going to call Catherine to have her join us, is that
OK Anthony?" "Great, ask her if she wants me to pick her up?" Emily
called Catherine and she was able to have dinner with us, so I told Emily, I
would go pick her up and we would meet her and Lou at the restaurant.
Emily asked if I needed directions to Catherine's and I said, I was good and
I left. I picked up Catherine and we headed over to the restaurant. I told
her about the deal I just made with Lou and Emily and she was excited
about it, but I got the impression that Emily had told her what they were
thinking. I did not tell Catherine about the cologne incident in Tahoe, I
really think it's better to keep that to myself, at least for now. We got to
the restaurant and we joined Lou and Emily at their table.

Emily greeted Catherine, "I'm glad you were able to join us for dinner
Catherine, but I asked Anthony if he needed directions to your home and
he seemed to know the way, do you have some explanation for that?" "I
guess he just has a good sense of direction." Lou jumped in to change the
subject, "Anthony agreed to take control of the house in Tahoe, isn't that
great news Catherine?" "Yes, when do you think you will start building?"
"I think that we should be able to break ground in 5 or 6 weeks, once I put
the team together." Emily proclaimed, "We all need to be there when we
break ground and celebrate, don't you think Lou?" "I think that will be
fun, I know the progress will be slow, but once we start, it will really feel
as though the whole thing is going to happen." The waitress came over
and brought the menus. Catherine spoke to the waitress, "You don't need
to give Anthony a menu, he already knows what he wants." Emily said,
"Why do you say that Catherine?" "Trust me, he just knows" "do you
know what you want?" Emily said with surprise. "Actually I do, so I really
don't need a menu" "I told you," Catherine said with satisfaction. Emily
was really confused, so Catherine had to explain why she was so sure I did
not need a menu. After Emily was satisfied with the explanation, we
ordered and had a good dinner and good conversation. I was getting
pretty tired, though, it had been a long couple of days, and it was time to

leave. We said our goodbyes, Emily sarcastically said, "Anthony, are you sure you can find your way back to Catherine's?" We all laughed and Catherine and I left. I took Catherine to her Condo and then I headed home. As I drove home, I was thinking about the project and how much work it was going to be, but it was pretty exciting. I was a little fuzzy on how much time I was going to have to spend in Tahoe, probable quite a bit, but it will be interesting to say the least.

When I got home, I saw Amy and Jim in their front yard, so I went over and asked if there was any information from Sid about the short term rental issue. They said they had another meeting and Sid talked to a city councilman and he said he would bring it up at the next meeting. I told them that that sounded like progress and then I went in the house.

I walked in the door and threw my keys on the table and sat down. A lot had happened in the last couple of days and I was going to need to get organized in the next 3 weeks, but I knew there was one thing I was not going to be able to avoid before I start Emily and Lou's home and that was trying to find Jenny's father. I knew that I could not put that off, so I decided that tomorrow I was going to put the effort in and get it done. I could really use Catherine's searching ability, but I was not going to get her any more involved, in fact I was very happy that the subject did not come up tonight.

In the morning, I went to get my coffee and since this day was going to be weird, I needed the Apple Fritter. "Good Morning Susan, How are you doing today?" "A little tired this morning, but I'm Ok." "Well, I'll have the Fritter with the coffee today." "Ok, give me a few and I will get it to you." I gave her $10 and then I left for the office to start my search.

First, I had a strange feeling, about Deena's house and the swing, so I wanted to see the records on the house and who has owned it through the years. I knew that this was not going to help me find "Walter Crane", Jenny's father, but I just had to get this off my chest. Tax records are public so I searched Deena's property. The reason that tax records for a property are public is that title companies have to search the title of every property when it is sold. They need to make sure that the title is clear at the time of sale, so every property has a trail. I have a real Estate Broker's license, so it is easy for me to search the property title. I pulled up Deena's property and it has had several owners through the years. I went all the way back to 1969 and there it was. The property was owned by Walter and Laura Crane. Laura was the name of the woman who said she was Jenny's mom in my dream. I just stared at the computer screen. They bought the property in 1969 and it was sold in 1973. The accident was in December of 1972, so it must have been too difficult for Walter to stay in the home after that so he sold it. It must have been such a horrible time for him, I have this empty feeling in my stomach just thinking about what he must have felt after the accident.

After I settled down a bit, my next search was to see if "Walter Crane" Owns anything now. I searched Orange County and Los Angeles County tax records. I put in his name and found a condo in Tustin, a single family home in Fullerton and another home in Downey, with the name "Walter Crane" on the title. There was no way for me to know which if any of these "Walter Cranes" is Jenny's father. There is no age on the records. The one in Downey shows a married "Walter Crane" The "Walter Crane in Fullerton is also married, but the one in Tustin is a single man. The only clue I have is that Jenny said that her father is lonely and sad. That could be any of these men, but maybe he is lonely and sad because he has no one and the owner in Tustin is single, at least that's what the records show. It was the only clue I have, but I am going to think about it before I do anything. I know that he would probably be in his late 60's or early 70's. The condo in Tustin has been owned by this "Walter Crane" for 23 years. The house in Fullerton has been owned by that "Walter Crane" for 10 years and the house in Downey has been owned by that "Walter Crane" for just 1 year. If I had to bet, it would be on the condo in Tustin, but it is still a long shot that it is Jenny's father.

My next search was going to be Social Media. Most people today put everything on Social media. So I entered then name "Walter Crane" and many people came up all over the world, so I narrowed the search. I tied "Walter Crane" Tustin California and nothing. I tried "Walter Crane" Fullerton and I got several places to search. I clicked on one and up popped "Walter crane, but looked like he was in his 40' so it was not him, but I wanted to see if he put his address anywhere on the searches but I was not able to find it. Since he was the only one who came up in Fullerton. I am going to think that he's the one on the tax record and not Jenny's father. I searched for "Walter Crane" Downey and several searches showed, but the picture that keeps popping up was a young man looks like early 30's so this was not Jenny's father. It looks to me that the best shot I have is the "Walter Crane" in Tustin.

The question now, is what do I do? Do I drive over to the Condo and knock on the door? If I do that, what do I say? These questions are not easy, but they will be for another day. I am going to put this aside for now and move on to other things. I know this is not going to go away, but the searches have given me enough to think about. I don't have to make any decisions now, but I do want to get this issue out of the way before I start the Tahoe project, so I don't have much time.

I had a few projects that I wanted to get finished up, so I went right to work and for the next 2 weeks or so, I am going to be very busy. Deena has not called, so unless she calls me in the next day or so, I will not be able to help her. It will take me a week to draw her plans and then take more time to get them through the city, so I really hope she does not call.

The days are going fast and I am working hard to get everything finished up. I decided to drive by "Walter Cranes" condo, just to see where it was. I didn't knock on the door though. I still don't know what to say. How do I even approach a man who I don't know, about a situation I am having with a little girl that might be his deceased daughter. This is not going to be an easy conversation. I don't even know if he will give me 30 seconds to try and get a few words out.

Keeping my word

We obligate ourselves without knowledge
We tell ourselves to be true
But obligation can bring uneasiness
When the task may be something
That we really should not do

May is almost over and I will be starting to work on the Tahoe home in a few days, so I decided to go to "Walter Cranes" condo and tomorrow is Sunday so it seems like a good day to go and see if I can get this over. It was time to see if the man who lives there is Jenny's father. I still don't know how I am going to approach him or what I'm going to say, but once I get there I will try my best to get my point across before he has me thrown out or worst. Maybe when I get there it will be obvious that he's not the guy I'm looking for, so If that's the case, I'm out of clues and I will have to put this behind me and move on. Of course, that may not be my choice.

I sat most of the night thinking about how to approach "Walter Crane" and try to explain the situation to him. I think I am just going to wing it. I could not sleep. So I walked to the park to see if I could get something, I don't know what, but in my time of need, Jenny is nowhere to be found. I would think that she would give me some sage advice, but I guess I'm on my own. I headed back home and caught a nap. My alarm went off a 7:00 AM and I took a shower and got dressed. I went to the donut shop to get some coffee. Susan did not work on weekends and the girl who was at the counter was new, and I had not seen her before. She gave me my coffee and I took off towards Tustin and the condo. I parked outside and just sat there for a while. There was no one in sight, so I got out of the car and walked over to the door. I was shaking a bit and very nervous. I still had no idea what I was going to say, but I hope if he is the right "Walter Crane" He would listen to me. Maybe I can get him to come to the park, Jenny wanted me to bring him to her and maybe he will come with me. I am trying to get up the courage to knock, but I walk away from the door and back to the truck. I sat and just tried to figure a way to do this. I got back out of the truck, I was sweating and very nervous, but I had to do this. I walked back to the door, lifted my hand to knock, but my hand just hung there. It was as if it was frozen in time, I could not knock. Finally I just did it, I knocked on the door. Nothing happened; no one came to the door, so I knocked again, but this time a little harder. I now heard someone coming towards the door and a voice yelled, just a minute!" It sounded like an older man so maybe it is the right guy. The door slowly opened and now it was time for me to try and get this conversation going. I now was looking at what may be Jenny's father. "The man at the door fit the profile perfectly. He was a tall, thin, grey haired man, with brown eyes and hunched over a bit. He looked like he was in his 70's.

"Hello, my name is Anthony, are you Mr. Crane." "Yes, I am Walter Crane, How can I help you." "Well Mr. Crane, I have something to go over with you and I need you to be patient with me because what I am going to tell you may seem crazy. First, just to let you know that I'm not out of my mind, I am and architect and have an office in Anaheim. Here is my card." "Can we sit on this bench here on the porch?" He looked at me like I was crazy, but there was something in his eyes that had him interested in a very cautious way. We walked over to a bench that was on his small porch. I was much more comfortable sitting outside and not asking to be invited in. "What is it that you want to tell me young man" "Have I ever met you before?" "No we never have met, but for the last few weeks, I have been going through something that may have something to do with you." I could tell he was confused and I did not want him to get scared and walk away so I thought I better get to it. "I was having trouble sleeping one night so I decided to take a walk. My clock read 2:34 AM, so I got dressed and started to walk. A warm "Santa Ana" was blowing so I threw the jacket that I had put on back in the house on a chair near the door. There is a park down the street from my home and I started to walk towards the park. As I approached the park, I heard laughter, so I continued to walk towards the laughter and I saw a small girl playing on the swing." "I'm Sorry; you said your name was Anthony?" "Yes" "Anthony, I don't see what this has to do with me?" "Please, let me continue, I know it's strange and you have been patient, but If you will indulge me a little longer, please." "Ok." "Anyway, when the little girl saw me, she took off. Now at 3:00 AM I thought that was a little strange, but I figured she snuck out of her home and then got scared and ran back home." "The next morning, I thought I might have dreamed it, but I saw the jacket that is usually in the closet, on the chair that I threw it on when I left for the park." "The whole thing bothered me so much, I even talked to one of my clients about it and she just thought it was a little girl that snuck out of the house." "The next night, I fell asleep in a chair and when I woke up, my clock again read 2:34 AM I really did not want to go to the park, but my curiosity about the 2:34 got to me, so I did go to the park and the little girl was again on the swing. I walked over to her, but this time she did not run away. She had short blond hair, green eyes and was wearing a long dress I watched her for a while and then I talked to her." I was now looking right into Walters eyes at this point and he was listening, but he was looking a little confused, I knew that the story was going to get a little harder for him, if he indeed had a daughter named Jenny. I continued. "I introduced myself to her, I told her my name was Anthony and she told me her name was." I paused for a moment; I did not know how he would react when I said the name Jenny. "Walter, she told me her name was Jenny!" At that moment, I knew I had the right "Walter Crane." His eyes welled up and he looked straight into the ground. " Why are you telling me this" "Walter, I had to find you, because for some reason I am being used by a little girl named Jenny for reasons unknown, I know this is hard for you, but please let me continue, please!" "Go ahead" I asked Jenny where her Mommy was and she told me, she was home with her brother. When I asked about her father, she said that she was taken away from her father and she became very sad and ran off again. I went to look for her across the park, but she was gone." I left on a business trip and when I got back, Mr. Crane, I then got a call from a woman named Deena who I knew 4 years prior and had not seen in two years. She wanted to talk to me about a room addition. I met with her and her husband and after I got home that night, I had a nightmare and in that dream I met Jenny's mother and her name was Laura." I stopped and Walter now got up and started to walk away. I was afraid I was going to lose him, so I quickly asked him if he ever used "Brut by Faberge" Cologne. Walter stopped and turned back towards me and asked, "Why did you ask me that?" "I had to take a trip to Lake Tahoe and I got a knock on the door. There was no one there and I walked outside my room to see If I could see anyone and when I got back in the room, There was an open bottle of "Brut" on the table. It was another dream, but I figured it had a meaning. So, I asked you again, did you ever use "Brut "Cologne?" He paused for a few moments, and said, "Yes, my daughter gave me a bottle on my birthday." At this point he sat down and then broke down. "He asked me in a very weak voice, why was I doing this. "Mr. Crane, I believe Jenny wants you to come to her. She told me you were lonely and she also told me the woman that I was with in Lake Tahoe was lonely, so she has been with me, even in Tahoe. She wants something from me; she wants me to bring you to her. The house that my friend lived in that wants a room addition was the home you owned in 1969. The old swing set was still in the backyard and there was a swing set in my dream. When I met Laura in the dream, she had a newspaper that was an "Anaheim Bulletin" and that paper has not been in business for years. The Headline in the paper was "Tragedy at Christmas Pageant." "Walter, I don't know why Jenny is using me, maybe I was just the guy at the park that night, I don't know, but I tracked you down, because I need to get to the bottom of this and I think you are the key."What is it that you want from me" Mr. Crane, I think you should come to the park with me, the park is right across the street where you used to live. I think if you come, maybe Jenny will be satisfied, I don't know, but I have tried to forget about this, in fact the woman that Jenny told me was lonely, begged me to forget about this, but I can't. That's why I had to find you. "Anthony, over 40 years ago, my family was taken from me, and I still hurt, but the hurt is bearable. 40 years ago, it was unbearable and I don't want to feel that way again." "I understand, could you at least answer a couple of questions for me?" "If I can." "What happened to "Sinbad?" "Sinbad was Jenny's dog, He died a couple of years after the accident, how did you know about him??" "I saw him in the dream." "Also, do you know what 2:34 might mean, it seems like I see that time everywhere." "It has no meaning to me." "Mr. Crane, You have been very patient and reasonable with me and I know what I have told you seems unbelievable and I never wanted to hurt you, but you have to understand that I am trying to fulfill what I believe your daughter Jenny wants from me." "The funny thing, Anthony is that I do believe that you are telling me the truth, but why you have been used, I don't know, but I am an old man and I just can't go with you, I'm sorry." "I understand, I just hope that I can put this behind me." Thank you Mr. Crane, and again, I am so sorry to have burdened you with this."

And with that I left. I did not know if I had done enough to get Jenny to leave me alone, or if she will continue to try and get me to bring her father to her, but I did not want to hurt that man anymore than I have already by bringing up those memories. I drove home and felt sort of relieved. I was not able to get Mr. Crane to come to the park, but I tried my best and I am going to have to be satisfied with that, because I am getting ready to start Lou and Emilie's home and I don't have time for distractions.

It's nice to have a friend

Having something on your mind
Can really take its toll
If you can share your story
A friend can help you bare your soul

I thought it would be a good Idea to let Catherine know what I did, because I did tell her I would keep her informed and meeting Mr. Crane should be the end of it. I asked Catherine if she had time to go to dinner tomorrow night and she agreed. After I hung up with Catherine, I was able to relax and watch a game. Tomorrow starts a new experience for me and I was excited to get rolling on it. I needed to put my team together because I would love to get the house built by Christmas.

I had a great night sleep and got an early start to the day. I contacted several contractors that I wanted to work with on the home and they all agreed to come to the office tomorrow to go over everything. I had "Cart Blanch" from Lou, so I can use anyone I wanted. I Called Lou and told him that I am now working on the home full time and he was happy about that. I headed home from the office; I was going to pick up Catherine at 7 PM, so I wanted to get cleaned up.

I headed to Newport and the traffic was pretty heavy, I thought about not telling Catherine about my meeting "Walter Crane," But I did promise her that I would keep her in the loop and in meeting with Walter, I think that may have ended this whole thing, whatever this whole thing is. I finally reached Catherine's and I walked up to her door. I heard someone behind me and it was Catherine. "I had to run to the store." She opened the door and I could smell that she had been cooking." I thought since you made pizza, that I would give you a sample of my cooking." "I never heard you talk about being able to cook." "Are you scared at what I might have made?" "No, well maybe a little." "You will survive." I waited in the living room while she finished and then she came to get me. "It smells good!" "I know you like shredded beef tacos, so I made them, I hope they are good." "Well, if they taste as good as they smell, I'm sure they will be great, you are a good listener." I took a bite of the taco and it was very good. "This is really good, I guess you can cook." We both laughed and since we were both in a good mood, I thought it would be a good time to tell her about "Walter Crane."

"You know Catherine, I am starting to work on Lou and Emilie's home and I wanted to get everything else out of the way." "Were you able to do that?" "I think I did a pretty good job of that and there was one thing that I have to tell you, but I have to admit, I thought about not saying anything to you. "Should I guess what it is, or does it have to do with a little girl." "You are right on the mark, I knew that if I was going to be able to move on, I was going to have to try and get this whole Jenny thing off my mind." "What did you do?" "Well, I found Jenny's father." "How did you do that?" "Before I tell you, are you sure you want to hear about it, I know you thought it would be better for me to drop the whole thing." "I still think it would be better for you to leave this alone, but I also had the feeling that you were not going to listen to me, so yes, I do want to hear."

"Well, the first thing I did was look up the tax records for Deena's home." Why Deena's home?" "Well, because of the swing in the yard and the swing in my dream, I thought there might be a connection." "How did you look up the tax records?" "Tax records are public and I also have a Real Estate Broker's license, so it was easy for me to do." "I didn't know you had a Broker's License." "Yes, so I found in my search that there were many owners before Deena, and, yes in 1969, "Walter and Laura Crane," Owned that house." "Remember in my dream, Jenny's Mother was named Laura." "Catherine, you look a little pale, are you sure you want me to go on?" "Yes, but it is getting a little scary," "I agree, but I knew that it was not a coincidence that Deena called me after not hearing from her for so many years." "So after I found out that Jenny's parents owned the home, I looked up "Walter Crane" on the tax records to see if he owned anything now. I found 3 properties with the name "Walter Crane," Then I searched Social Media to see if I could eliminate any of them and I was able to eliminate two of them and the "Walter Crane" who owns a condo in Tustin, was my best shot. He had no Social Media footprint, so the only way I would be able to know if that was him, was to go to the property and meet him." "That's pretty good detective work," "Yea, I could have used your help, but I did not want to involve you any more than I did." "You know, Anthony, I'm not that fragile, I would have helped." "I know, but I just did not want to upset you," "Ok, well what did you do next?" "I knew that this was still a long shot, but I drove out to the condo, just to see where it was and then I sat all night thinking about how to approach this. Yesterday, I decided to go, so I drove back out to the condo and walked up to the door, but I could not knock, so I walked back to the truck and sat there for a few minutes to get my courage back. I walked back to the door and finally knocked. When a man answered the door, he fit the profile of age. He was tall and grey haired and he looked like he was in his 70's." "Now, my problem was, how do I start. He had a bench on a little porch outside his condo, so I asked him if we could sit on the porch and he agreed. I slowly got into the story and at one point he asked how it pertained to him, I just asked him to indulge me and he did, so I went on. When I got to the part that I named Jenny, he started to get emotional and he started to walk away, so I knew I was starting to lose him, so I used one other bit of information that I had that I had not shared with anyone." "What was that? Catherine quietly asked." "When I was in Tahoe a few weeks ago finishing up the plans, my first night there, I went to bed and I was awakened by a loud knocking on the door, I got up to answer the door and there was no one there. I walked outside and notice some activity, so I went to see what it was, but it was just a group of people, so I went back to the room. I noticed the clock read 2:34 and then I found an old, open bottle of "Brut by Faberge" Cologne. I had no Idea where it came from, but with the time on the clock, I thought it must have had to do with Jenny. The thing was Catherine, it was another dream, so when Walter started to walk away, I asked him if he ever wore that brand of cologne. It was a very difficult moment and he came back and sat down and we talked some more. He told me that his daughter gave him a bottle on his birthday." "That sounds so sad." "It was very hard, but I knew that since I had come this far, I had to ask him if he would come to the park with me. I told him that Jenny wanted me to bring him to her, but he declined. He said that the pain that he went through 45 years ago, he did not want to revisit. Even thought he still feels the pain of that night, time has made it bearable for him and he just can't come with me. I understood, but I had to ask him if 2:34 meant anything to him, but he said no and then I apologized to him for bringing this to him and I left." "Anthony, That had to be an unbelievable experience, I could not have done it" "Catherine, as hard as it was, I knew I had to try and give Jenny what she wanted. I did that and I think it's over now." "How can you be so sure?" "Nothing is for sure, but I can't do anything else, I have done everything I could do, so it has to be over." " I really hope so, for your piece of mind" "It's time now for me to move on and starting Lou and Emilie's Home, with the travel and everything else that I have to do, I have to put this behind me." "Well, I give you a lot of credit; I know that had to be hard." "It was, but I have to say, when I left Mr. Crane's, I felt like a weight had been lifted off my shoulder, I just hope that he was Ok after everything I told him. All this has happened to me and I still really don't understand what it's all about, so I can't imagine what he was thinking."

"Not to change the subject, Catherine, but these taco's are really good." "I'm glad you like them, I made plenty, so enjoy." "When do you think you will be able to break ground in Tahoe?" "If I am able to get all my contractors up to speed, I think we should be ready in 3 or 4 weeks." "I will probably have to go back to Tahoe this week with the grader and the plumber, that way I can get the first step ready and once I do that, then I will know more." "Are you planning on coming for the ground breaking, Catherine?" "Oh yea, Emily is already planning the party," "As soon as I get a date, I will let you know so you can arrange your schedule." "That would be great, thank you." "It's the least I can do for someone who can make shredded tacos like you!" "Yea, I can never forget how important food is to you." "How long do you think it will take you to finish?" "If we can get started, end of June, first part of July, I am hoping to get it done by Christmas, but don't mention that to Emily, I don't want to get her hopes up, with a project like this, things can change." "Are you looking forward to the travel back and forth?" "No, not really, but I have come to grips with it and I will try to get as much done while I am out there, to cut down on the travel, but realistically, I will be there quite a bit for the next 6 or 7 months." "Did you have to turn down any other work?" "I finished everything that I started and Deena never called, so I had a clear slate and I think it will be better to just concentrate on the house in Tahoe."

I'm happy that I told Catherine, I told her I would keep her informed and now that I think the situation is over, she should not have any worries. I knew that she had strange feeling about the whole situation, it almost seemed as though she was afraid of a ghost that may or may not exist, although, I now am pretty sure she does exist.

Let the fun begin

You draw it in a room
Your mind creates the scene
But bringing those plans to life
Will grow from dirt to the finished dream

It is now June and I was really excited about getting the house started. I talked to everyone I needed to talk to and I scheduled a trip to Tahoe in two days. I wanted to break ground by late June or at the latest early July. I decided to use all Nevada contractors, Even though I would have liked to use people that I was more familiar with, Doing business in another state can be tricky and it is better to use people who know how the local inspectors work, plus there are license issues, so I am trying to keep it as simple as possible.

I landed in Reno and met the Grader and the plumber and we drove up the mountain and started to map out the first phase of the project. We decided to set a ground breaking date for June 24th. I decided on that day, because it was a Saturday and I knew that Lou and Emily wanted to be there for the ground breaking. The next day I met with the concrete contractors and also the framers, and the roofers. The project was starting to take on a life of its own. I finished with my work and I drove to Reno and headed home. When I got home, I called Lou and told gave him the ground breaking date. He was excited and said they would schedule a trip. I then Called Catherine and let her know, that way she could arrange her work schedule and be there for the ground breaking.

The days were moving quickly and I had no time for anything else. Unfortunately, I got a call from Deena and she said she was ready to get started on the room addition. I felt really bad, that I had to tell her that I could not do it. She understood. I told her that I could recommend someone, but she said that they may wait until I am able to do the job.

It was now June 22nd and I was ready to leave for Tahoe. I wanted to get up there a couple of days ahead to make sure everything was still on schedule. Lou, Emily and Catherine were coming up tomorrow. This time, I would be staying in Tahoe for at least 2 weeks and maybe longer. Once we break ground, I want to make sure that everything keeps running smoothly. The first phase of any project can be a little tricky and I want to be around in case anything comes up.

I made it up to Tahoe and went right to work, I was pretty excited and I confirmed that everything was on track. I told myself that I would stay away from the casino until the project was over, so I got something to eat and headed back to the cottage. I fell asleep watching an old movie on TV. I suddenly woke up and the clock read 2:34 AM. What woke me up was perfectly clear, I had another dream. This dream was not nightmarish though, it was actually cheerful, now that I am awake I realize, that me thinking that I could just put everything aside and move on was not my call. In the dream, I was driving down the street near the park. There was a big banner outside the school. "Christmas Pageant Tonight," The next thing I knew, I was standing in the back of the room, watching the performance. I could see Jenny singing Christmas songs and Walter and Laura Crane, sitting in the front row. They all looked happy. When the performance ended, Jenny walked up to me and said, "I love Christmas, don't you?" With that, I woke up. I remember Jenny saying that to me once before in the park. What was the message of this dream? I tried to get her father to come to the park with me, he declined. There was nothing else I could do and I just don't want to deal with this anymore. I was pretty angry now and I just yelled out, "Jenny, I know you can hear me, you have to leave me alone now, I did what I could for you, but I can't help you anymore. You should go to your father, but you have to do it without me, I'm done!" After I finished my rant, I just sat down and waited, for what I don't know. Maybe she would show her wrath, but nothing happened. I turned on the TV and after a while I fell asleep. When I woke up, I thought about the dream again, maybe Jenny was just trying to let me know that she was happy, now that I spoke to her father. Maybe I was reading it all wrong. I don't know, but I am really tired of the whole thing. I am way too busy to have this on my mind, so I am going to do what I can to ignore it and make believe the dream did not happen. Good luck with that!

Lou, Emily and Catherine were due to arrive today, so I did some work and then waited for them at the cottage. When they arrived, they were really excited. I told them that everything was on schedule and we would be breaking ground at 8 AM. We could not start any earlier, due to the local regulations. I drove them to the lot and showed them how everything was laid out. A construction site before the ground breaking is like a blank canvas, before the artist begins. All that's there is emptiness and dreams of what will be. The fun part about a project like this is to take pictures of the whole process. You can see the project come together, day by day and piece by piece.

We headed back to the hotel and had dinner. I told them that I made a promise to myself to stay away from any gambling until the project was complete. They all laughed and said they don't think I can do it. I told them, that I will do it and I have great will power. I don't think I convinced them. Lou told me that he will be in the casino and he will let me know how the dice were treating him. He got great pleasure out of taunting me. While Lou was in the casino, Emily, Catherine and I went out to the pool area and talked. Catherine asked me if I was nervous about the ground breaking. "No, I am just anxious. There is so much work to get to this point and it just feels real good to get started." Emily said she was nervous and can't wait until the home is built. I told them that I will be staying in Tahoe for at least two weeks and it may be longer, depending on how things are progressing. Catherine asked If I needed her to drive to my home to make sure everything was Ok every once in a while. I told her that if she is ever in the area, I would really appreciate that. I told her where the hide key is. She told me that she is in the area all the time and would be glad to check it out. I Thanked her.

Emily then popped in with a suggestion, "You know Catherine, while Anthony is away, we could go to his house and then go over to the park and see if we can find his little friend." I just looked at Catherine as she replied, "I think we would have to go very early in the morning, but the little girl probably only has eyes for Anthony." "What's wrong Anthony, you have gone quiet, are you afraid we may chase your ghostly girl away, knowing that she has competition for your affection." "No, I just worry that she my take the two of you away and we may never see you again. Maybe you should stay away from the unknown; I would not want Lou to have to share this new home with a new young girl friend." "If that happened, I guarantee, there would be a very unfriendly spirit creating as much Chaos as possible," We all laughed. Then Emily yawned, "I think I will go find Lou and go to bed." "Good night, see you bright and early in the morning." As Emily walked away, Catherine said, "You know Anthony, You did get pretty quiet when Emily brought up going to the park. Is there something that you haven't told me?" I just looked down, trying not to look Catherine in the eye. She seems to be able to read my body language. "Come on Anthony, let's hear it." "Well Catherine, you know I have been trying to keep you out of this and I thought the whole thing was over, but I did have another dream last night," "What was the dream about?" "I was driving by the school by the park and there was a big banner, "Christmas Pageant Tonight" The next thing I knew, I was standing and watching Jenny singing in the pageant and her two parents sitting in the front row." "It was actually a very happy dream, but at the end of the dream, Jenny walked past me saying "I love Christmas, Don't you, and then I woke up." "I remember she said that to me once before in the park." "I remember you thought that was strange." "Yes, but after I woke up, I got angry and yelled at her, that I could not help her anymore and she has to go away." "Do you think that will work?" "I have no Idea." "You know Anthony, I know you told me to not think about this, but I think we are missing something and it may have to do with the 2:34. I have been doing some reading on spirits and it seems as though you are dealing with a friendly or benevolent spirit." "Oh really, do they say that these friendly spirits can be a pain in the ASS!" "Well, they say that many times these spirits don't know that they are dead, or they may be sending you a message." "Catherine, I thought I knew the message, but I could not get her father to cooperate with me, In fact, after thinking about it, I think I did the wrong thing, by bringing up painful memories for the poor guy," "Maybe, but I also read that if multiple spirits are wanting something from you, then they can be relentless. Remember in your dream, Jenny and her mother wanted you to help them bring the father to them. "Great, they may be teaming up on me." "Yes, and I also read that you probably were not picked at random. There is a reason they picked you. There is something about you that they know and whatever that is, they want to use that knowledge to help them." "Well so far, I have been a failure and for the next few months, I don't have time." "A couple of other thing that I read, First, the spiritual encounter can be in person, or a dream, but if the spirit manifests itself both ways, then the connection is strong, and second, if a spirit is following you from place to place, then no matter where you go, that spirit is going to show up. Most spirits stay where they are comfortable, but they can move with you if they feel as though they need to." "You know Catherine, for a person who is supposed to be freaked out about this; you have done some real research on it." "It does give me a queasy feeling, but it also makes me curious. Doesn't it make you a little uncomfortable Anthony?" "Sometimes, I think that the whole thing is just my imagination." "Really, how can that be?" "Well, maybe I read something about the accident when I was younger and it for some reason hid itself in my brain and is now coming out." "Ok, how do you explain Deena and the home she lives in, and how do you explain the cologne?" "Well, I can't and the funny thing is that Deena called me and wanted to go ahead with the room addition, but I had to tell her I can't do it. She told me that they may wait until I can do it." "That's interesting, what if Jenny did not want that swing set torn down and now it's not going to be." "It will be torn down eventually." "Yes, but maybe after she gets what she wants." "I don't know, Catherine, but there is something more important." "What's that?" Well, you are leaving on Monday and Sunday, there is no work going to be done, so we should do some spring skiing. There is still snow on the mountain." "Amazing how you can switch subjects, but since the snow is there, I agree, we should take advantage of it." "Great," "I have one other question Anthony." "Yes" "Why are you staying away from the casino until the home is complete?" "I am here to work and Gambling to me is not to win money, but to amuse myself, so I only want to do it when I am on Vacation." "That will really take some self control." "Yea, but I am all about anticipation and the buildup of events. To me the excitement of thinking about something that is going to happen, can actually be as much fun as the actual event, so putting off entertaining myself with gambling makes the anticipation of it when the home is complete a lot of fun and when I do throw the dice, it will be much more satisfying." "I think I just learned quite a bit about how your brain works." "Scary isn't it?" "Just a bit."

I walked Catherine back to her Cottage and then I drove out to the lot, just to think about what is about to happen tomorrow. I am real excited for Lou and Emily and I'm glad they are going to be there to celebrate the event. Just sitting in the car and looking out at the view from the lot to the Lake, It is going to be a beautiful home when it is complete. It's funny, as an Architect, I have drawn many homes and looked at them when they are complete, but now, since I am technically building the home, I feel much closer to the project, almost as if the home is a part of me.

I decided to go buy two nice bottles of Champagne, so Emily can break one over the backhoe, before it starts to dig the footings. I'm sure she will get a kick out of that. I bought the second bottle in case they wanted to drink it. I know I won't be getting much sleep tonight.

Christen it with one bottle or two

Champaign will make the bubbles flow
Perfect for ringing in a new year
But bubble can flow in other ways
To Christen and bring on happy tears

The morning has come and I drove out to the lot. Lou, Emily and Catherine will be here in about an hour. I of course will wait for them before we begin work. The backhoe operator is here and ready to go. I see Lou's rental car driving to the lot. The lot sits up a slight slope, so from the lot you can see the road below. Emily comes running out of the car, "I'm ready, lets "break ground". "You can feel her excitement. I said, "Hold on Emily, we have to "Christen" the lot before we start." I handed her the Champaign and she walked over to the backhoe and broke the bottle, yelling, "LET THE BUILDING COMMENCE!" I don't know what I did with the second bottle of Champaign; I must have left it somewhere. With that the backhoe started up and the ground was pierced and the building has begun. There was a lot of excitement, but watching the footing being dug is fun for about 10 minutes and then it becomes boring, so the three of them took off for breakfast. After a while, they came back to see if I wanted anything, but I was pretty busy with scheduling and making sure everything was going according to the plans and to be quite honest, learning on the job, so I told them I was good and they left.

After a full day of digging, we made good progress and the plumber is set to come out Monday to put in their pipes to get them ready for inspection before we pour the foundation. We should have the forms and the plumbing ready for inspection by Wednesday. I headed back to the Hotel about 6:30 and met with Lou to give him an update on the progress of the day. It was a pretty exciting day and really could not have gone better. We agreed to meet at 8:30 for dinner and I went back to my cottage and got cleaned up.

We all met at the restaurant and Emily was still excited. Catherine told them that she and I were going to go skiing tomorrow and Lou said that they would be golfing. I was really looking forward to having a day of skiing, because I know that it probably will be the last day for me to relax for a while, and spring skiing is the best. The Hotel was having a poker tournament and Lou decided to go and play for a while after we ate. Emily and Catherine went to a show and I just hung out at the pool and made a few calls to set things up for Monday. After their show, Catherine and Emily came out to the pool area and we talked for a while. Lou met us there after he lost in the poker Tournament. We went to the coffee shop to get some late night desert and coffee. Lou and Emily went to bed and Catherine and I made our plans for tomorrow. We were going to have to rent skies again, so we wanted to get an early start so we could have a full day of skiing. We both headed back to our cottages and turned in.

I met Catherine at her Cottage at 9 AM; we got some breakfast and headed to the ski area. We rented our equipment and were ready for the ski lift. It was a beautiful day and the snow was very good for this late in the year. It was a little slushy, but still very nice. We skied for 3 hours and then decided to get some lunch. We were both having a great time and Catherine told me that it's going to be hard to go back to work after such a nice weekend in Lake Tahoe. We finished our lunch and headed back to the ski lift. We got to the top, and I heard Catherine call to me, "Anthony," Anthony." "What's up Catherine?" "Look over there at the little girl with the racing vest on." I turned to my left and about 50 yards away, was a little girl wearing a racing vest with the number 234 on the back. They were having races for small children, but the difference was that all the numbers were from 0-99; this little girl was wearing 234. "Catherine, I have to go see who that little girl is." I started to ski towards her and she started to ski down the mountain. I picked up my speed so I could catch up with her. The little girl was skiing along the tree line going at a pretty good pace. I did not want to lose her so I was really moving, also following the tree line. The mountain was starting to lean to the left and as she turned the corner, I lost sight of her. But once I turned the corner I am able to see her again. My skis now are pointed strait down the mountain and the wind was pounding on my face. The snow was soft and slushy and I could feel my right ski starting to shake. Not wanting to lose the little girl, I kept going even though if felt as though my ski was about to give way. All of a sudden my right ski hit an edge and went flying off and I went tumbling down the mountain. It felt as though I rolled for 100 yards before I finally came to a stop. I got up and looked, but the little girl was gone. Catherine skied down to me. "Anthony, are you Ok?" "Yea, but I lost her; these rented skies could not take the speed of the run." "Anthony, I saw her ski between those tree's about 50 yards ahead." We both skied in between the trees and down to a rest area. Ahead of us was what looked like a play area for kids and a red swing set? "Catherine, Look at the swing." The middle swing was moving back and forth as though someone was on it, but it was empty except for a ski vest. We skied to the swing and I picked up the vest and it was the one the little girl was wearing. It had the number 234 on it. Then on the ground to the right of the swing was a bottle of Champaign. The same brand of Champaign that I bought for the Christening. Catherine said, "What is the deal with the Champaign?" "Well Catherine, I bought 2 bottles to bring to the lot, but I could not find the 2nd one, I thought I just misplaced it." "Anthony, she is telling you that she is with you no matter where you go." "I guess she is and it looks like getting mad at her the other day had no effect." "You know Anthony, I think she has a plan and she is going to do what she has to do to get you to help her." "What are you going to do?" "You know what Catherine; I am going to do my best to ignore her. I have too much to do and I don't have time to play this game." "Do you think that it is going to be possible to ignore her, she seems to have a very persistent disposition?" "Oh, Catherine, She's no different than most women, sometimes you just have to pretend they are not there." We both laughed," Well, I'm glad to see you still have your sense of humor." "I'm glad you also have a sense of humor, Catherine." "Now that you have seen her for yourself, Catherine, how does that make you feel?" "A little scared, I'm shaking a little." I went over to her and gave her a big hug. "I don't think she means any harm; I just think she wants something." "Come on, let's get out of here," I put the ski back on and we went down the mountain. Our day of skiing was over and we turned in the rented equipment and headed back to the hotel. I was a little concerned for Catherine, until today, Jenny was just an idea to her, but now that she has seen her with her own eyes, I could see that she was affected by that. The drive to the hotel was a quiet one and I walked her to her cottage. We talked a little and then I left. We both met Lou and Emily for dinner and then Catherine and I went and sat by the pool, while Lou and Emily took in a show. "How do you feel now Catherine?" "Ok, but I am worried about you and what Jenny has in store for you." "Don't worry, I'm sure that she will invade my dreams, but If she brings me harm, she will lose her chance of getting what she wants from me, and I don't think that's what she is all about." I walked Catherine back to her Cottage and I could see she was shaken up. "You know Catherine; I think we should find a good movie to watch on TV. What do you think?" "I would like that" "It will probably be late when we finish, why don't you pick up a few things in your cottage so in case you fall asleep, you have what you need and don't have to go out in the cold." "Ok, you sure you don't mind?" "Of course not, and you can even pick the first movie," "That's a deal." I could see Catherine was relieved that she did not have to be alone and I was happy to have some company to watch a movie. I was upset, though that this was all my doing, getting Catherine involved with the whole Jenny thing. Hopefully, when she goes back home, she will put all this out of her mind. Catherine picked the first of two movies we watched. About halfway through the second movie, she fell asleep. After the movie ended, I woke her and she went to bed, I stayed in the other room.

In the morning, I had to get up early and get to the lot, so I quietly showered and left before Catherine woke up. I knew that they were leaving this afternoon, so I thought instead of Lou renting another car to drive to Reno, I would finish my work and drive them. I called Lou about 9AM and told him what my plans were and he agreed. Their flight was at 5 PM, so we would want to leave Tahoe about 2:00. I got back to the hotel at 1:00 and showered and got ready to drive them to Reno. I heard a knock on the door and it was Catherine. "Thank you for last night, I'm sorry I fell asleep on you." "No problem, did you sleep well?" "Yes, surprisingly I did, I felt bad you slept on the couch though."

"You know I never sleep." "Oh, that's right, I forgot." "We both laughed and she said, "Emily said you are going to drive us to Reno." "Yea, I thought it would be better than having Lou rent another car." "What time are we going to leave?" "In about ½ hour." "Ok, I better go and pack, I will see you in a bit." I drove them to Reno and we had time to get some lunch before they had to leave. I pulled Catherine aside and told her that if she needed to talk to call me any time. She said that she will and then they all boarded the plane and left for home.

Now that the work has begun, I was really focused on making sure that everything stayed on track. The days went by fast and we now are in August. The home is framed and the roof is on. I take pictures every day and frequently talk to Lou about the progress and send them the pictures. Catherine seems to have gotten over the Jenny thing; we talked about it a few times, but not in a couple of weeks. They all are planning to come up here in September and by that time, we should have the outside of the home wrapped and the inside work in progress. I still think we should be done by Christmas, but I realize things do change. I thought that I would have gone back home by now, but I have been so busy, I have not wanted to leave. I am really enjoying the whole process of the building of the home. I think that being so busy, I have been able to ignore the Jenny situation, and I rarely think about it and have not had any sightings or dreams since the ski episode. Whatever her plan is, it seems to be on hold, at least for now. I have kept my goal of staying out of the casino, until I finish the project; I just work, eat and sleep. Working in Lake Tahoe and building on a lot that is right on the lake, makes things very pleasant.

It is now September and Emily, Lou and Catherine are coming to see the progress of the home. Lou and Emily need to start to make some decisions on appliances and paint colors. We are not quite ready yet, but the time is coming soon. Catherine had checked on my house a few times and I asked her if she could bring me a few things, she said she would. I am looking forward to seeing everyone, it has been a while since I have spent time with anyone other than construction people and them coming up will give me a reason to take a little time off. Emily called me the other day and told me that Catherine had a

Birthday coming up next week. She has helped me so much, since I have been away, that I wanted to get her something that she would like. I remembered that she told me while we were skiing that she needed to get new Ski's and Boots, hers were very old and not worth restoring. She told me that she liked "Salomon" equipment, so I bought her "Salomon" Skis, Boots and Bindings. I have the equipment here with me, but we can go tomorrow and get her the right size and style she wants and they will ship it to her home. I wanted her to know how much I appreciated the time she took for checking on my house and of course being my sounding board for the whole Jenny thing. They were going to be here in a couple of days and I think they will be surprised at how different the home now looks. Yes, I have sent pictures, but seeing everything in person will make a real impression on them.

Whispered in the Wind

The wind blows in silence
Yet it seems to speak to me
I listen with great interest
As it tells me what the future may bring

It was Thursday September 7th and my phone rang and the ID said it was Deena. "Hello Deena, How have you been, Are you a Mommy yet? "Yes, I had a little boy and we named him "Walter" I could not believe what I heard, so I repeated what she said. "You named him "Walter?" "Yes, it was a little strange, but Larry and I were sitting in the back yard one day talking about names and the wind started to blow. As the wind blew through the trees, we both heard the same sound, "WWWAAALLLTTTEEERRR." We heard it over and over, the same sound. We both said the same thing, if we have a boy we need to name him "Walter." "Weird huh?" "You don't know how weird that is Deena, You heard a sound from the wind and you named your son after that sound." "You always knew that I am a little strange." "I will remain silent on that." "That being said, I am calling to see how your project is coming." "It is going well; I have been in Lake Tahoe working on it for the last couple of months." "Larry and I have decided to wait for you to finish, so you can help us with our room addition, if you still can." "Of course, but it will probably be the first of the year." "No problem, "Little Walter" is not in any hurry." Hearing her say that again gave me the chills. She named her baby because a spirit told her to and she didn't even know it. "Deena, how is Larry doing being a new Dad?" "He loves it, he was a little nervous as the time got closer, but once he held "Little Walter." He was in love with the idea of being Daddy." "That's great, how did you come through the whole thing." "I was scared, but I was ready and everything went pretty well, no complications and a very healthy baby." "It was funny though, When I was in the room after I gave birth, Larry had just taken the baby to see the doctor a few doors down, and a little girl came in my room and whispered to me that my baby was beautiful, and that she heard his name was "Walter," And that was her father's name. She told me that her name was Jenny. The strange thing about the little girl was that her eyes were a beautiful green and I could see my face when I looked into them. She told me that she was going to go play on the swing and then she left. I asked the nurse who came in right after the little girl left, who she was and the nurse had no idea what little girl I was talking about. She said children were not allowed on that floor." "Strange, Anthony, don't you think." "Well maybe someone snuck her in to visit someone." "Yea, I guess, but her eyes." "Well you know Deena; your eyes are pretty nice also, so you now know how it feels to look into mesmerizing eyes." "I guess so." "I am very happy all went well for you, and as soon as I get back, I will call you and we can start on your room addition." "That would be great; I will look forward to hearing from you." "Goodbye Deena."

After I hung up the phone, I had to sit down; Jenny visited Deena when she had a baby. Why did she want Deena to name her son after her father? After so many years, why is Jenny doing all this. Maybe she has just come back from beyond and now wants to be with her father, or maybe it has something to do with "Walter" and the situation he is in. I just don't understand, but Jenny seems to be going through a lot of trouble to get something done. I know one thing; Jenny has some kind of plan. She used me to talk to her father and also had Deena buy her old house, call me to help her with a room addition and name her new baby Walter. WHY?

I don't know what it all means, but it gets stranger and stranger every time something new happens. Now there is a baby named "Walter." It was time for me to get something to eat and get back to the Hotel. I found a little deli a couple of weeks ago; it's not as good as "Tony's," But not bad. I got myself a sandwich and then back to the cottage. I told myself not to think about my conversation with Deena and I tuned on a Baseball game and tried to relax.

I got up early and wanted to get to the lot and finish a few things. Lou, Emily and Catherine are going to be here in a few hours and I wanted to meet them back at the Hotel. Before I left the site, I made sure that everything was clean and safe for Lou and Emily to take a tour.

I got to the Hotel and Lou was already there. They called me and I told them I would see them in a few. When I got there, I told them that we should head back to the lot so they can see their home. Catherine came with me in the truck and Lou and Emily drove their rental car. We got to the lot and Emily ran to the house. She was so excited about how far the place had come in a short time. The sun was still out, but it was starting to set and the view from the window of the home was breathtaking. Even though the home was a long way from being finished, it was now far enough along that their dream house was looking like a reality and in a couple of months or so, it will be. They all took the tour of the home and we stayed inside the shell of a house for about an hour. I answered many questions and told them that tomorrow we should go over some things that they are going to need to make decisions on soon. We headed back to the hotel and I got cleaned up for dinner. While we were at dinner, Lou sarcastically asked, "So Anthony, how have the Crap tables been treating you?" "Lou, I have not even thought about the casino's, your home is the only thing that I have occupied myself with since the last time you were here." "Do you really expect us to believe that you have become a house hermit?" "Believe it or not, I have been so busy, and focused that it's even good to see your face." We all laughed and of course Lou headed to the casino after dinner and Catherine, Emily and I, went to the pool and just hung out and talked. "Anthony, the home is really coming along." Emily said excitedly. "I have looked at every picture you sent, but seeing it in person and being inside the home itself is just an amazing feeling, thank you for all your hard work." "I am really enjoying it." "Catherine would not let me come with her when she checked up on your home, I guess she was afraid I would rattle the spirits." "No, I was just afraid you would try and redecorate the place before he came back." "You're probably right" Lou found us at the pool. "I'm broke for the night. You know, Anthony, seeing the house, I believe you have been working too hard, so I want you to take these two days off while we are here." "I accept that order, it will be good to not think about anything for a couple of days." "Well," Lou explained, "we are going to head for bed." Then Lou and Emily left. "You know Catherine, we should watch a movie, I'll let you pick." "Ok, I will try not to fall asleep like the last time." We headed back to the Cottage and she picked out a move. "Catherine, before we watch the movie, I heard you were having a Birthday soon." "Emily and her big mouth, right." "I'm not saying anything, but I am very grateful for your help since I have been gone and I wanted to get you something for your birthday, I hope you don't mind." "You mean you got me a gift?" "Yes I did and I hope you like it." "Ok, when are you going to give it to me, I'm excited now." "I thought I would give it to you now, if you'd like." "I would like" I went into the bedroom and brought out the packages. "Wow, that's a pretty big package." She tore the wrapping paper and Yelled "OH MY GOD" "These are beautiful; I can't believe you did this." " I really hope you like them" "I really love them" "That's great, We need to go tomorrow and get you the right size and any style you want, I just wanted to have these here for you to open." Once you get the ones you want, they will ship them to your home." Catherine walked over to me. "Thank you so much." And she gave me a very nice kiss. "Well, if I would have known that you were going to react that way, I would have given you something a while ago." We both laughed "Now Catherine, we can watch the movie." Catherine again fell asleep during the second movie. I'm beginning to think that one movie is her limit. I helped her get to bed and I left her to sleep the night away.

In the morning, Catherine got up and she said "I did it again, Huh?" "Yea, you are a movie light weight, one and you're done." "I have some coffee here if you would like it." "Oh yea." "I am so excited about my new skis, I wish there was snow on the mountain." I think you will have to wait a couple of months, but after breakfast we can go and get you the right size." "That will be so nice, thank you again." "It is my pleasure."

We met Lou and Emily at their cottage and Catherine told them about the skis. Emily was going to come with us to the store, but Lou wanted to do some gambling. We finished breakfast and we left for the store. When we got there,

Catherine picked her style and size skies and Boots and they set her bindings. We had them pack everything up and they were going to ship them to Catherin's home. I took Emily aside and thanked her for giving me a heads up on Catherine's birthday. We then headed back to the hotel to meet up with Lou.

We all headed over to the house and even though I said that I was going to not think about the house for a couple, I had to go over things with Lou and Emily, so they could start making some decisions, I did not want things to slow down by having any delays. I gave them information that they could take with them, and then we left. The weekend went too fast, but I had to get back to the reason I was out here and that was to get the house finished. Before they left, Catherine ask me if I was going to come home any time soon, and I told her that I would be back for Halloween. I like giving away candy, and I hope she will help me do that. She said that she would and they left. I decided to keep the conversation I had with Deena to myself, at least for now and I was determined to ignore any dream or other ghostly encounter.

The days are starting to get shorter and it is getting colder, but the house is continuing to make progress. It was now the middle of October and I was planning on being home for Halloween. I really like Halloween, I guess it come from when I was young and going "Trick or Treating" and just having a good time. Now I just enjoy giving out candy and watching other people enjoy the day. Who knows, maybe Jenny will make an appearance for Halloween.

Let all the Monsters come

The night is eerily silent
I have a creepy feeling inside
Monsters, Monsters everywhere
Could Halloween night be close in sight

I was very excited to finally be going home. It has been a long time, I actually never thought I would be away that long, but things are going so well that I did not want to stop, so I just stayed in Tahoe. I will be home for several days. It's very cold in Tahoe and the weather has not been good, so it is a real good time to get away. I landed in Orange County and was surprised to see Catherine waiting for me at the Airport. She wanted to save me the trouble of getting a ride home and I really appreciated it. She told me that she was looking forward to Halloween and she was going to get dressed for the occasion.

Halloween night was here and Catherine was dressed as a very tasteful "Maid Marian." I do not dress up; I just watch others get dressed. We had a very busy night and many kids coming to get their candy. I am always amazed at some of the older kids that go "Trick or Treating." Catherine had a good time and I told Kher to just stay over, so she did not have to drive home on Halloween night. After Catherine went to sleep, I had an agenda. I decided last night that I was going to go to the park at 2:34 AM and see if Jenny was at the park. Part of me thought this was a very bad idea, but the curiosity was much too strong for me to ignore it, after all, it is "All Hallows Eve" and it is said that the veil between the dead and the living is very thin on this Halloween night. I checked to make sure Catherine was sound asleep and I headed to the park. It's funny, but after all this time and all the things that have happened with Jenny, I was very relaxed, almost as though Jenny was a friend, even though for all I knew, she could also have been a foe. It was a cool night, and kind of overcast. The scene was perfectly set for a ghostly encounter. The neighborhood was quiet and as I reached the park, there was no one in site. I did not hear any laugher like I did before and I headed to the play area, but no Jenny playing on the swing. I guess she is a no show tonight. Maybe she is haunting someone else for Halloween. I sat on the swing in the play area and just contemplated Jenny and what she really wants from me. It was a little spooky sitting on the swing, though and I thought it might be a bad idea. I looked at my watch and it was 3:00 AM. I looked around and there was no one anywhere, I started to get out of the swing and I heard "I Knew you would be here" I turned around and there she was. Jenny was wearing the same dress and looked as she always looked. "I wanted to see you and I thought tonight would be a good night." "You have tried to run away from me." Jenny said softly. "No, I have been working, but I noticed that you have not let me get away from you, why do you sneak around, you know you can talk to me." "You don't understand anything, Anthony" "No Jenny, I don't, why don't you tell me." "I have told you, I asked you to help me, to help my father, and you told me you would." "I told you I would try and I talked to your father, he still misses you and your mom and I feel bad that I brought those bad memories back for him to think about." I can't do that to him again." "You will." "No, Jenny, you have to understand, I can't." "You must." "Tell me Jenny, why make Deena give her baby you fathers name, why put that in her head? Deena told me you visited her after her baby was born." "You need to tell me something." "I will tell you something, the lady you are with tonight." "Yea, what about her, she doesn't know yet but she will, she will know before you." "Know what." "You need to leave Catherine out of it." "I want nothing from her, she wants to help you, she is very smart and knows where to find the answer, but she just has not found it yet." "Jenny, you have done a lot of work to put this whole thing together, using Deena and me, but what I don't understand, is why can't you just go to your father yourself?" "You don't understand, but you will." "Look at me Anthony, What do you see?" "I see a very sweet little girl who is not of this world." "No, you see the light that will light the way." And with that last word, she was gone. This time, she did not run away, she was just gone. I know nothing more now than I did before I came here tonight and what did she mean, "She is the light, which will light the way."

Confused and tired, I walked home. Jenny was not scary to me, she was just confusing. She still wants me to help her with her father, but I can't and hopefully, eventually she will move on. I got home and sat down. A light went on and it was Catherine. "You went to the park, didn't you?" "I did, the night was made for a ghost story." "Well did you get your story?" "Come over here, Catherine and sit, I want to tell you a ghost story. I did see a ghost tonight, and we talked and I am more confused tonight then I was before." "She also said that you know where the answer is, but you just don't have it yet." "What does that mean?" "I don't know, but when I told her to leave you out of it, she said she has nothing to do with you, you are trying to help me and you will know the answer before I do." "Then she said something really strange." "What?" She asked me to look at her and asked what I saw. I told her that I saw a very sweet little girl that is not of this world." She said, "No, you see the light, which will light the way." And then she was gone. "Anthony that is a ghost story." I then told Catherine about Deena and the name of her baby and how Jenny visited her. Catherine then asked," Anthony, What is Deena's married name. "I don't know when I looked up the tax records, I did not look at his name, and I was just interested in Walter." "Can we look now?" "Sure, let me log into the site." I pulled up the records and there it was. "Catherine, you're not going to believe." Before I could finish, Catherine jumped in, "His name is "Crane, Isn't it?" "Yes, Larry Crane, the same last name as Jenny." "Anthony, you know that means that there is another "Walter Crane" in the house since the baby is named "Walter" "This is just unbelievable. Jenny is manipulating everything, I wonder if Larry is a relative of Jenny." "I will bet he is, Jenny brought Deena and Larry together somehow, Anthony, do you know how they met?" Yes, Larry told me when I went to the house for dinner, He said, and you're not going to want to hear this, but they met at a funeral." "Your kidding, whose funeral?" "Some guy they both knew from Larry's work." "Anthony, I'll bet the cemetery they were at was the same one that Jenny and her mother are." "That I don't know, but it makes sense." "Oh My God, Anthony, I think I know why the name and the house" "Really?" "Just hang with me on this; didn't you say that Jenny had a brother that was also killed that night?" "Yes" "What was his name?" "I don't know." "I think that Jenny feels as though her father was robbed from having a legacy when his family was killed that night and she has now put together a new "Walter Crane "Legacy. That is amazing." "You know Catherine, Jenny said something else about you?" "Do I want to know?" "She said you were very smart, and it seems as though she knows you pretty well." "I'm not sure that having a ghost call you smart is a good thing." "She may think I'm smart, but I still can't put together what she wants you to do to help her with her father, and that is the real mystery." "She said you would figure it out before me and I'm sure she is right." "Anthony, now that we have been talking about Ghosts on Halloween, I don't think I can sleep." "You know Catherine; I know what will make you sleep." "What's that?" "Let's find a movie to watch, you will be out before it's over.""Very funny!" "I thought it was." "Ok, but I pick the movie." "What's new about that, but Have you thought that the reason you fall asleep is that the movies you pick are boring." At that point, Catherine picked up a pillow from the couch and threw it at me. "Ok, Ok, I take it back, go ahead and pick a movie.

The next day, Catherine asked me what I was going to do about Jenny, and I told her that I was going to ignore her and go back to Tahoe and finish the house. I was actually heading back to Tahoe in a couple of days so Jenny will have to wait. We drove to Lou and Emily's house, so I could get their decisions on certain things that are ready to be done to the house and we went to dinner, I told them that the next time they see me, the house will be done, At least that was my plan. I told Catherin, when they do come for the house warming, to bring her skis, because the snow should be great at that time.

Back to Tahoe, One last time

You have worked so hard
The task has been long and fulfilling
As I sit and wait and think
In the end the whole thing is more than thrilling

I'm sitting on the flight back to Reno, just thinking how far I have come in the last several months. There was a point where I thought I would never get this project done. I remember when I did not see a light at the end of the tunnel, but now I do and I'm very excited to get back and get it done. I do know, though that the hardest part of anything is finishing, and for the next month in a half, I will be working on finishing this home. I would be lying, if I tried to tell myself that I could just ignore Jenny and all that has come about on that front. I can't believe that this little ghost or spirit has been such a force since I met her in the park back in April. I have so many questions, but those questions I hope will wait, but will they? I am hoping that Catherine puts the whole thing out of her mind, but I don't think she will. I do think that she is right, Jenny manipulated Deena's life in order to get a legacy for her father and for some reason, and I have been chosen to be her conduit. Did Jenny pick me, and then need Deena to pull me deeper into the story, or was Deena, or her husband picked first and I was just a convenient pawn. That question may not ever be known. I do know one thing though; I have my work cut out for me starting tomorrow.

The weather is now very cold in Tahoe. It should be, it's November and there is some snow on the ground. The good news is that most of the work for the house is inside, so the weather is really not an issue. I ordered the appliances that Lou and Emily wanted and I talked to the painter and let him know what colors that will be needed. Looking at the home from the outside, it really is beautiful. It looks like a large, modern, mountain cabin resting in the middle of large pine trees and a fantastic view of the Lake and the snow capped mountains. The area here is very quiet and at night, the stars are magnificent to see. The most peaceful way to enjoy the area is to take a small boat out on the lake at night and just sit there and take in the whole mountain. It really makes you feel insignificant when you see the majesty of this place. They say that there are areas of the lake that they don't even know how deep it is. The people, who live here, are not people who need to work, though. There is very little work in this area, unless you work at the few hotels here or maybe have a small business. Many people, who live here, work for the city in some capacity. Of course Lake Tahoe is split between Nevada and California. Most people want to live on the Nevada side, for financial reasons, but just being able to spend the time here the last few months, has really given me an appreciation of the area. When you come here just for a visit, you really can't get a flavor for the mountain.

Thanksgiving is getting close, but I am going to stay up here through the holiday. The house now is so close to being complete, I just want to get it done and to leave for a few days and come back, will just delay things. The appliances are in and most of the painting is done. Now the hard part, putting in the pretty stuff, the crown molding on the ceiling and all the "Ginger Bread" around the house. I figure if things continue to progress the way they have been, I will be done around the 8th of December and that way, Lou and Emily can come up for that weekend and have a nice winter house warming party. Catherine called me the other day and wanted to know if I was coming back for Thanksgiving, but I told her I was not. She will be spending Thanksgiving with her children; she told me that they are all going to Lou and Emily's house. Knowing Emily, they will have the whole thing catered. I did tell Catherine my plans to have the house finished by early December, but not to tell Lou and Emily yet, until I'm sure. I don't want to get their hopes up and then disappoint them.

At first, working for Lou and Emily was a real pain. I was thinking that they are the reason that I actually met Jenny that first night. I was so frustrated with the way things were going with the plans and changes, I had to take a walk to the park to clear my head. It's funny, I hadn't thought about that night for a while. Thinking about my walk to the park that night, I can still feel the warm wind blowing and I can hear the laughter from the park. I wonder why Jenny ran away that night. I don't know, but even thought the first part of working for Lou and Emily was frustrating, they have turned out to be great people to work for and good friends. I hope they enjoy this house for many years to come. I will never forget this experience. Now that I think about it, it has opened up a whole new way for me to look at my business. I am not just a guy, who draws plans, but I now not only create the building, but I actually build it. I really have Lou and Emily to thank for that.

Well, the day has finally come. I have called for a final inspection today and if all goes well, I can let Lou know that his house is complete. Now I know that there will be things that Emily will want done, but getting the final from the city makes this a real home. I dialed Catherine's number; I wanted to let her know. "Hello Anthony is everything Ok." "I hope so; I am waiting for the inspector for the final inspection.""You must be out of your mind with excitement!" "I'm pretty excited, but I don't want to get ahead of things, in case they will want something else done." "Have you told Lou yet?" "Not yet, I want to give him the good news once I get it signed off." "I know they are very excited, they have been looking at the pictures you have been sending them." "What time is the inspector going to be there?" "Between 8 AM and 10 AM." "Waiting must be hard, is anyone there with you?" "No, I'm just sitting here all alone." "Poor baby. Call me when it's over, Ok." "I will, as soon as he leaves." "Good luck, but I don't think you will need it." "I will take all the luck I can get." "Bye." I am really happy that Catherine has become such a good friend. Not only has she helped me with things I needed while I was away, but being able to talk to someone about the Jenny situation has been a big help. I do worry a little about her involvement, although I believe it when Jenny said she has nothing to do with her. I do wonder what Jenny meant when she said that Catherine will know the answer before I do.

The waiting is driving me crazy. I see the inspector driving up the drive way. He is a pretty nice guy. It has been the same inspector throughout and that helps. "Hello Jack, how are you today, I hope you are in a good mood." Jack is a burly man who has lived in Tahoe his whole life. As inspectors go, he is a good one, he never surprises you with crazy requirements and he seems to understand how hard it is to build out here in Tahoe. "Hello Anthony, I guess you want to get out of here and go home." "It will be good to get home, it's been a while." "The house looks great, let me go through it and I'm sure you will be good." "When are you leaving?" "The owners want to have a little house warming, maybe this weekend, so I would imagine, after that." "Well, good news, give me that inspection card, so I can sign you off." "You know Jack, let me get a picture of you signing that, I want to keep that as a reminder." "Sure, just make sure you get my good side." "Here you go Anthony, all signed sealed and delivered." "Thank you Jack, You know, you should come for the party, you have been with me the whole time." "We are not allowed to do that, but I appreciate the offer." "I understand, thank you very much." "No problem, it's a beautiful home you built, you should be very proud." "I am thank you." "Hope to see you around, have a safe trip home." "Goodbye Jack."

After he left, I called Catherine and let her know, and then I called Lou. "Hello Lou.""How's it going up there, Anthony?" "Pretty well, I just e-mailed you a picture, do you see it." "Yea, what's that guy signing?" "He's signing your final inspection card, the home is done." "Oh MY God, let me get Emily." I heard him yell "EMILY, EMILY, Come here, quick. "What's going on Lou?" "Here talk to Anthony" "Hello Anthony, what's Lou yelling about." "Look at the picture I sent him." "Ok. Let me see Lou." "Emily, that guy is signing your final inspection card. Your home is complete and finalized." "I think I'm going to faint" "Lou, "take the phone while I catch my breath." "You really knocked her off her feet, Anthony. You did a great job; we are going to come up for the weekend, so we can have the house warming." Are you OK for a couple of more days to wait for us?" "I still have a few things to do and that will take me a few days, so, yes, I will be fine." "Great, we will be there Friday." "Anthony, you need to go out and have good time tonight." "Lou, I will wait for you and we can hit the "Crap Tables" You got it Anthony" "See you guys Friday." "Goodbye, Anthony and thank you so much." "You are very welcome, Goodbye Lou." That felt really good, I could hear their excitement. I can't wait until they see the home on Friday.

My phone rang, it was Catherine. "Anthony, Emily just called, she is so excited and can't wait to see the house." "You know Catherine, the snow looks real nice on the mountain, and I think we need to get on the slopes." "My skis are already packed and ready to go." "You must be exhausted after all the work you did?" "I'm Alright now; I'm just relieved that it turned out so well. You know there is always the little voice in the back of your mind that tells you that things might not work out so well, but I guess that little voice was wrong." "I guess so, but you know that Lou and Emily never had a doubt about you and the job you were doing, and neither did I." "Thank you for that, it means a lot." "Are you going to celebrate tonight?" "No, I'm going to wait for all of you to celebrate." "Not even a little casino run?" "I told Lou, we would hit the "Crap Tables" When he gets here." "That will be a lot of fun, since you have stayed away from the casino for all this time." "That is the one thing that Lou did not think that you would be able to do, to stay out of the casino, but you did." "I did, and I'm happy I did, it will be so much more fun, now that the job is done." "I will see you Friday, Catherine." "I am looking forward to it." "Bye"

Lou called me back and wanted to see if I can have the hotel cater a little party on Saturday night. He also wants me to invite all the people who worked on the house. I told him I would take care of it. I called a cleanup company to come out and make sure the home was perfect before everyone shows up on Friday. I also had a landscaper come out and asked him to put some nice flowers out. They will not last because of the cold, but he will put them in on Friday morning and at least they will be good for a day or two. I then went to the Hotel and set up the party for Saturday.

Let the party begin

Excitement is in the air
The showcase is ready to see
Everyone will be impressed
But it all means so much more to me

Friday is here and I am very excited to see the reaction of Lou and Emily when they see the house. I am starting to realize that the house is more than a house to me, it is my creation and I feel a pride in it, that I did not have any indication I would feel. I went to the house to make sure everything is looking good. The landscaper is there putting in the flowers and they really make the place look nice. The inside is cleaned and smells great. It has the new house smell, which is sort of a paint, hardwood smell. I think tonight, at the party I will be kind of a tour guide and I will love every minute of it!

I will start by taking people through the huge double Dutch front doors, and then we will enter into the massive entry that sports two very beautiful and expensive paintings on each side. On the right side past the paintings is a huge picture window that has a great view of the mountains. The entry has an incredible travertine floor that continues throughout the house and it butts up against an 8" plank hardwood floor. I talked them into having a mix of travertine and hardwood, so that the hardwood floor would be well preserved. The travertine is used as sort of a pathway throughout the house and then is surrounded by the hardwood. Most of the traffic will be on the travertine and that will keep the hardwood looking great for years to come. There is also not a stitch of carpet in the home. I talked Lou and Emily out of carpet. I hate carpet, because it gets so dusty and dirty. If Emily wants carpet, she can put nice area rugs in specific areas of the home.

As you pass through the entry, you come to a magnificent living room, with a vaulted exposed beam cedar ceiling and four huge ceiling fans high on the beams. The room is mostly windows with views of the lake and mountains. Right now, the mountain peaks are covered with snow and looks just increasable. In the center of the living room, there is a round fire pit that has seating around it, like you would see at a ski resort. The furniture will not be here until Emily picks it all out. The lighting is a mix of wall sconces and recessed lighting that dim when you want low light. Walking past the living room is a kitchen that any chief would go crazy over. There is a 15' center island with Pendant lighting the full length of the Island. The Island also has the most beautiful color granite counter that I have ever seen and that same granite is throughout the kitchen. The island also has a prep sink and custom cutting board. There is a huge "Sub Zero" refrigerator and Freezer, with a "Wolf" range and also a "Wolf" double oven of course a microwave, dishwasher, there is also a 2 sided fireplace on the opposite wall of the range and the other side is the dining room. The kitchen also has a view of the Lake and Mountains. Before you walk into the dining room, there is a 10'X5" wine closet, which is decorated with beautiful natural stone.

The Dining room has a vaulted exposed beam cedar ceiling that is surrounded by a huge sliding door that when opened, opens up the entire length of the room as if you now are dining outside, sitting about 20' away from the beach. There of course is the fireplace that is the other side of the kitchen fireplace. There are ceiling fans the entire length of the dining room with lighting. The walls are big and made with large paintings in mind. The dining room leads to a family room that again is surrounded by windows that overlook the lake and there is a French door that leads to a huge covered patio that has a fire pit and a wood burning Pizza Oven. . There is also a full wall fireplace that is made out of river rock. You walk through a windowed hallway and you come to The Master bedroom that is raised up so it is able to have a 360 degree view of the Lake and Mountains and the French door, leads to a private beach area. There are two offices connected to the master and there are two master baths that are connected with a double sided fireplace and both have Jacuzzi tubs and large rock showers. The sinks are vessel sinks with waterfall faucets. The master also has a kitchenette.

There are 4 other bedrooms that each has a bathroom and each have a fireplace. Going towards the rear of the home, you walk through a windowed hallway that leads you to a guest house that has two bedrooms and two baths both with fireplaces and a living room with a fireplace and a kitchen.

The exterior of the home is surrounded by a walking deck. You can walk the entire perimeter of the home and it is covered by an overhang to protect against the weather. When you drive up to the front of the home there is a roundabout driveway that leads you to a covered carport area that has room so you can park 4 cars. You walk up the 30' walkway to a huge covered porch with a fire pit. Eventually there will be plants and trees along the walkway and porch. In the rear of the home there are 4 patios and all of them have fire pits. Each patio is covered with lighting and ceiling fans and heat lamps. The Garage has room for 4 cars and also has an office for Lou. The exterior of the home is made of pressure treated wood that is made specifically for harsh weather. The color is a natural color. The landscape lighting surrounds the entire home and eventually when the landscaping is done, the lighting will be strategically placed. The home sits above the road and is a ranch style single story that sits on 1 acre of land. I know that I will be giving many tours this weekend.

Lou just called and said they are at the Hotel. I told them I was at the house, so they will drive over and be here in a few minutes. My excitement was building as I was getting ready for my first and most important tour. I see the car coming up the road and then up the driveway. I meet them at the carport out front. I can see the excitement in their eyes. "Ok are all of you ready for the grand tour" Emily ran up to me and gave me a huge hug. "I am ready Anthony." Catherine said," I think Anthony is just as excited as we are to give us the tour." "You are so right Catherine." I walked them through the home, pointing out all the amenities and answering all their questions. Emily was thinking about furniture and artwork. She told Catherine that they were going to have to do a lot of shopping in the coming weeks. After the tour, Lou and Emily were speechless."Anthony, it is more than we imagined" Lou said. Emily got very emotional and said, "You know Anthony, when you and I were designing the home, I had ideas about what I wanted and I know I drove you crazy with the changes and revisions, but you really turned the ideas into reality and I just can't even believe what you have done." "We can't thank you enough." "No thanks necessary, but you should know that this home is like my first born, so I am much attached to it." "I was thinking earlier today that I am so surprised how much I really have a feeling for the home." Lou jumped in, "Anthony, I can only imagine how you feel."

I told them that the hotel is going to bring seating, tables and the food for the party tomorrow night. All the Fire pits are hooked up to the gas from the home, so they can just be lit. Emily asked how many people will be showing up and I told her about 25. She was excited about having her first party, even though her furniture is not here and the decorations are not here. I told her that the people who will be here for the party could care less about that. I did walk around to the neighbors and invite them, I hope they come. They all said they would. Emily said she was going to invite a few people from the hotel that they have gotten to know.

Emily and Lou went back to the hotel, I think they were a little over whelmed. I had a couple of things to do and Catherine stayed with me. "You know Anthony, I have known those two people for many years, but I have never seen both of them get so overwhelmed before. I have seen Catherine get emotional, but Lou is sort of a rock." I know, it makes me feel real good and I know that they will enjoy showing off the home tomorrow night."

As we were driving back to the Hotel, Catherine asked me if I was excited about going home. "I am ready, Catherine, I have been here a long time and at times it was pretty overwhelming, but it's time to get back to my regular life. But I will miss this place and I know that I am going to miss this home." "I do want to say one thing to you Catherine; I really appreciate you helping me in so many ways while I was gone. It would have been much harder for me to stay away as long as I did, if you were not there for me." "You mean by me helping you, I kept you away." "I guess so." "I'm glad I could help, but I'm really looking forward to skiing on Sunday." "Just look at the snow on the mountain," "Yea, I have been looking at that snow for weeks, so it will be so nice to actually be able to play in it."

We got back to the Hotel and Lou wanted to meet for dinner in an hour, so I got cleaned up and we all met at the hotel restaurant. When you go out to dinner with Lou, he will never let you pick up the check. I try every time and he just grabs my arm and will not let go until I give up and give him the check. Usually he just gives the waitress the credit card before he even sits down, but in this Hotel he just tells them to bill his account. For the money he has spent at the Hotel in the last year, they should be buying his dinners.

We finished dinner and Lou wanted to go to the casino and I was ready. My moratorium was over. The Crap Tables were calling. Catherine and Emily hung with us for a while, but then they got bored and left. Lou and I were there until 3 AM. We both lost and then dragged ourselves out of the casino and into the coffee shop for a snack. We talked about the house and the party and since its 3 AM, the party is actually tonight. After we had our snack we went back to the cottages.

I woke up at 7 AM, showered and headed to the hotel lobby to check and make sure everything was going to be ready for the party tonight. I was pretty excited to show off the house and I know Emily and Lou were also pretty excited. I headed over to the house with the workers from the Hotel and let them in so they could get started setting up. My phone rang and it was Catherine. "Good morning Catherine, you are up early this morning." "Your one to talk, where are you?" I'm at the house with the hotel people setting up for tonight." "Did you even sleep at all, Emily told me that Lou got in at 3:30 this morning and he like a normal human is sound asleep." "Well, I had to make sure things were ready and I never told you that I was normal, or human." "I'm starting to believe that." "Are you going to come back for breakfast?" "I will head to your cottage in about 30 minutes," "Ok, I will let Emily know." "Ok, see you in a few." I made sure everyone knew what they needed to do and I headed back to the hotel. I Picked up Catherine and we then met Lou and Emily at the Restaurant. I told everyone that everything is in the process of being set up for tonight. The food will be there at 6 PM. "Anthony," Emily asked, "I don't know where you get the energy, When Catherine told me that she called you this morning and you were at the house, I was amazed how you were even standing up. I had to pry Lou out of bed after you two gambled until 3 AM, How do you do it?" "I don't know, I guess I am still running on adrenalin." "Don't let him get away with that Emily, He never sleeps, I think he is a Vampire or something." "Catherine, I don't think I want to be known as a Vampire, Can't I be a Pirate." "What does a Pirate have to do with not sleeping?" Emily said with some sarcasm. "Well a Pirate is too busy chasing women and pillaging the towns to sleep." Lou jumped in, "Oh, let him be a Pirate if he wants, Emily." "Ok, you are a Pirate that does not sleep." "Great, maybe someday I will have a Pirate ship and a crew." We finished breakfast and I told them that I was going to head back to the house. Catherine asked if she could come with me and I was good with that. Lou wanted to go back to sleep and Emily was going to meet with an art dealer to talk to him about paintings for the house.

Catherine and I headed back to the house to make sure the preparations were going well. The people just about had everything set up. Catherine told me that Emily invited several more people, so there may be 35 or 40 people there. We should have plenty of food and drink to handle the extra people, so I was not worried, the more the merrier.

We headed back to the hotel to get dressed for the party, and we got back to the house at 5:30 PM. No one was there yet, so I took one more stroll through the home before the crowds came. Lou and Emily came and they were dressed very elegantly. Emily was wearing a long blue dress with 3 inch pumps and a leather jacket. Lou, actually had a tuxedo on, but he told me that it was just for show, he brought a change of clothes. I went around the house and lit all the fireplaces and fire pits. The food showed up and the party was ready to go. The sun was setting and with the fire pits going and the beautiful backdrop of the lake and the mountains, the home was really a sight to see.

I gave tours of the home all night and Lou and Emily were like proud parents telling the story of how everything came together over and over. As the party started to wind down, It all hit me at once, that the months of work and sacrifice was over and what had been accomplished was spectacular, but it was just a memory now and I was going to have to get used to a going back to a normal life back home.

The ripples in the lake

As I stare out at the Lake
The beauty is without compare
But what message can be discerned
As the ripples in the lake appear

Lou and Emily were wiped out and headed back to the Hotel. The people from the Hotel cleaned up everything and were heading out. I was standing on the patio, just staring out to the Lake. "Catherine, Why don't you Take the truck and go back, I think I want to stay here tonight." "You want to say goodbye, don't you?" "I guess I do," "This house has a spirit to it that I just can't explain and I have to just sit here and take it all in." "I understand, but could you use some company?" "Sure, But there's nothing here for you to sit on." I don't want you to be uncomfortable all night." "I'll be fine." "I know what we can do, I can take the seats out of the truck and we can use those to sit on." I went to the truck and pulled out the seats and set them up in the living room taking in the magnificent view and with the fireplace roaring, it was very comfortable. I felt bad that Catherine was not going to get a good night's sleep, but she insisted that she was fine. We talked about the house and I told her stories about what went on and about 2 AM she fell asleep.

I was just staring out at the lake and I felt a warmth behind me, at first I thought it was just the fireplace, but then I felt a hand on my shoulder and I turned to see who it was and it was Laura, Jenny's Mother. I got a real strange feeling, I had gotten used to Jenny, but her mother, who I only saw in a dream. "Beautiful, isn't it." I was still in shock, "What is beautiful?" "The view, it is really beautiful, I can see why you stayed away so long." "I was working." "I know, Jenny told me, but you know you can't run from your obligations." "What obligations, I don't understand?" "She enjoys spending time with you, you're lucky, she will miss you." "Miss me, what does that mean, I'm going back in a couple of days." "You're talking in cryptic riddles, both you and Jenny want something, but you will not be specific. You just throw out things and expect other people to understand, well I don't understand and I have no obligations to you or Jenny. I have gone out of my way for you and I even hurt your husband by bringing up bad memories, so if you are trying to help him, it is not working. Maybe you picked the wrong guy!" why did you pick me to fulfill your desires that is a real mystery to me." "We all have desires and obligations, Anthony, your path is set, but you are fighting it and as long as you fight it, the reasons will remain in darkness. My husband has had so much taken from him, but his brother's son has fulfilled his legacy, now you need to fulfill yours." "Do you really think this is all about what we want?" Before I could answer, Laura opened the big door and ran out and jumped into the lake and was gone. I was mesmerized and could not take my eyes off the lake. The moon was glistening off the top of the water and the only movement was the ripples that were caused when Laura jumped in. I waited to see if she was going to come up. But she didn't. The big door was now open, so I caught a chill and I got up to close it and I tripped and hit the floor. I was in a daze, and when I looked up to clear my head, I was staring right into the fireplace. I looked back to see if Catherine was still asleep and she was. I looked at the big door that Laura opened to run out, but it was closed now. Could this have been another dream? Why was it Laura this time and not Jenny? What did it mean when she said that she will miss me? Was she talking about Catherine, or Jenny, or someone else." I don't know, but I think it was time to head back to the Hotel, so I woke up Catherine and we walked to the truck and headed back to the hotel. Catherine could not find the key to her cottage, so I told her to just take the bed in my cottage. I could not get Laura out of my mind and what she said. Yes, it was probably a dream, but I still think it was their way of getting a message to me, even though I don't really know what I can do for them. Maybe, because I am going home, I just had the Jenny on my mind and that's why I had the dream. Will this ever end, or will I wake up and this whole thing will be a dream, Jenny, Lou and Emily, Catherine and the house. Maybe none of it is real and it's all a weird dream. Now that would make sense to me, because the rest of it does not.

I fell asleep in the chair and when I woke up, I thought about the dream, or whatever it was. I looked in on Catherine and she was still a sleep. I took a shower and got dressed. Catherine and I were going to go skiing, so I drove over to one of the local ski shops and rented my ski gear. I figured if I did it now, it would save time. I drove back to the Cottage and Catherine was getting some water from the fridge. "I was too tired to ask last night, but what happened; I thought we were going to stay at the house." "Well, I was worried that you would be uncomfortable and I realized we were going to go skiing, and I wanted you to get some rest." "You couldn't find your key, so you just slept here." "Did you sleep Ok?" "Yea, I slept fine, what time did we get back here?" "About 3 AM." "Ok, let me get cleaned up and we can get some breakfast and go skiing." "Ok, I will go talk to Lou and Emily and let you get dressed." I headed over to Lou's cottage and we decided to meet at 9 AM for Breakfast. I got Catherine and we headed to breakfast. Catherine told Lou and Emily how we stayed late at the house last night, just enjoying the view and taking in the spirit of the home. Emily told me how much she enjoyed the party and thanked me for setting everything up. We finished Breakfast and Catherine and I headed to the slopes.

It was a beautiful day and the sun was shining and snow looked great. Catherine was very excited to try out her new skis and she carefully took them out of their case and stepped into them. I asked "How do they feel?" "They feel so good and they look great." "They really do look good; now let's see how they ski." "We sat on the lift and headed up the mountain for our first run. I still had Laura on my mind, but I was trying to forget and just enjoy the day. I don't know when I will be able to get back here to ski, so I really want to enjoy it.

"So Anthony, Now that your big job is over, are you going to take some time off." Maybe a few days, just to get used to not being in Tahoe, but I do have Deena's plans to work on and a couple of other jobs that may be just around the corner, so I don't think I will be enjoying the life of leisure any time soon." "Before we reach the first run Anthony, I wanted to talk to you a little about the 234 number that you keep seeing." "Well. It's not just a number, it's the time." "I think it may not be the time, I have been trying to find something about 234 that may give you a clue." "Have you found anything?" "Not yet, but I am going to keep looking." "Well, Catherine, I don't want you to lose any time on it. I'm sure this will go away soon." "It's funny, last night, I was thinking that maybe all of this is a dream." " What do you mean a dream." "Don't laugh, but what if we are not really here, the house, Tahoe, Skiing, everything that has happened in the last several months has not really happened at all, and I will wake up and that will be it." It's all just a figment of my imagination." "Well, Anthony, as much as I would like to be considered a dream, I am really here and so are you, so I hate to disappoint you, but it's not just a dream." " I told you not to laugh." "I'm not laughing, I can imagine how distraction something like this must be." Yea, but I can't let it become such a distraction, that it gets in the way." "I understand, Oh, I forgot to tell you, I called my cell phone company and got the voicemail to text on my phone and I love it." "It's great isn't it?" "Yea, but you are right. Sometimes is does not understand what is said and writes some crazy word that does not make sense." "It can be pretty funny, but it usually just missed a letter or if a word sounds like another word it gets it wrong, but for the most part it is pretty good." "Ok Catherine, are you ready to ski." "Let's go"

The first run was great and the rest of the day went real well, but now it's time to go and tomorrow, back home. We got back to the hotel and got cleaned up for dinner. Lou, told us he thought he was going to play golf, but Emily had him go with her to shop for furniture, I could tell he was not real happy with that. "Anthony," Lou said with hope," Are you sure you want to go home, you could stay and help Emily decorate." "No Lou, I think I will leave that to you. Decorating is not really my cup of tea." Catherine explained, "Unless you want your house to look like a Bachelor pad." I laughed, "What are you trying to say, Catherine." "You don't like my decorating skills?" "I would never say that." Lou jumped in. "That sounds good to me, what do you think, Emily?" "That's Ok, Catherine and I will take care of the decorating, Thank you." "You know Lou, I feel as though I has been disrespected here, what do you think?" "I agree, I think after we eat we should go drown our sorrows at the Crap Table." "That sound real good." Lou and I did just that for several hours and then It was back to the cottage, pack everything up and get some sleep.

Home sweet home

Is it really time to go
I have been away for so long
But as I think about what will be left behind
I have to wonder where I really belong

The morning has come and it's really time to get ready to go. I am thinking about how much I have changed in the last 6 months and how much building the house has changed my career. I know that I will never forget this experience and the memories of taking this house from paper to completion. I have a very satisfied feeling, but I am a little sad also. Getting up every morning and going to the house and working on it was a very fulfilling feeling and of course being in such a great place make it even better. Going back to draw plans for Deena's room addition does not really excite me right now.

I have loaded all my stuff in the truck and am ready to go. I wanted to drive by the house one more time, just to take one last picture. I just realized that with all the pictures I took of the home, there was not one of me standing in front of the house. I knocked on Catherin's door, hoping she would come with me to take the picture. "Good Morning Catherine, I have a favor to ask." "What's up." " I just realized that I don't have a picture of the house with me standing in front, could you come with me and take the picture." "Sure, I knew you couldn't leave with saying one last goodbye." We drove to the house and took several pictures and then went back to the Hotel where we met Lou and Emily for Breakfast. The plane was leaving at 2 PM. So we had about an hour before we had to leave. I we checked out of the hotel and headed down the mountain.

Catherine drove with me. We boarded the plane and took off and my Tahoe adventure was over. We landed in Orange County and then Home.

I brought all my luggage in the house and put it in the living room. I will deal with it tomorrow. I went back out to get a couple of other things and Amy saw me and came over to talk. "So are you home for good, or are you leaving again." "I am home for good." "How did everything go?"
Great, did anything exciting happen while I was gone?" "Sid has been working on the city to get the short term rentals to stop, but so far he has not had much success, but he still feels like he is going to get it done." "I hope he does." "Ok Anthony, I will let you get some rest." "Goodnight Amy."

Amy was right, I did need to rest. I sat down and turned on the TV. I fell asleep in the chair, but the sleep was not a restful one. I woke up at 2:34 AM and I was a little excited, not because I was home, but because of the dream that I just had. It started again with me driving by the school and seeing a big banner outside the school saying, "Christmas Pageant Tonight" Then I found myself again standing in the back of the room, watching the pageant. There was Jenny singing on the stage with the other children, and then I saw her mother Laura sitting in the front row, but this time Jenny's father, Walter was not with Laura, he was with me in the back, and he was holding Deena's baby. I woke up and the reason the dream excited me, was that I think I now know the answer to the puzzle.

I thought about things the rest of the night and at 8 AM my phone rang, it is Catherine. "Hello Catherine." "I wanted to know how your first night back felt." "Ok. I fell asleep in my chair, so I guess I was pretty tired." "I'll bet you were, after being gone so long, your body will need a few days to get used to being home." "I guess so, Are you working today?" "No, I am taking a couple of days off." "Good, How about I pick you up for lunch; I really don't want to start unpacking yet." "Ok, what time?" "How does noon sound?" "Great, See you then." "Goodbye."

It was true, I did not want to tackle the unpacking and the laundry and putting everything away. I will leave that for another day, but the real reason I wanted to see Catherine was to tell her what I think the whole thing is about. I did want to go to the office first and see if there was any mail I needed to address, so I drove over and sat at my desk. I thought I should call Deena, but I really didn't fell like it, I will do it tomorrow. The mail was mostly junk and there was nothing that was important, so I locked up the office and headed to Catherine's. When I got to Catherine's, she said that she knows I want to go to In N Out, since I have not had it in a while. I appreciated that, so that's where we headed. We ordered our food and found a table in the patio. It was a very warm December day and Christmas was in the air. I started the conversation about Jenny and why I now think I understand. "Catherine, I think I understand what Jenny wants from me." "Tell me." "Well, last night, I had a dream, remember the dream I told you about with me at the Christmas Pageant." "Yes, I remember." Last night, I had the same dream, but this time, it was a little different." "What was the difference?" "I still saw Jenny singing, and her mother Laura in the front row, but Walter was standing with me in the back, holding Deena's baby." "Really." Yes, and I think that's the answer." "What's the answer?" "I think Jenny and Laura want me to bring Walter to meet Deena's baby." "How are you going to do that? He already told you he does not want to think about the whole thing again." "I don't know, but there has to be a way." "Wait, I just remembered something." "What's that?" "I didn't tell you this, but the night we were at the house and you fell asleep, I had a dream that Laura came to me and she said a lot of stuff, but the one thing that I just remembered is that she said, that her husband's brother son has fulfilled his legacy." "What does that mean?" "What if Walters's brother had a son and that son is Deena's husband and fulfilling his legacy is by having a baby and naming him "Walter." "That's a big if, don't you think." "Maybe, but there is only one way to find out, I need to go to Deena's and ask." "Let me call her now" I called Deena and told her I was back in town and if she is home, could I come by and take another look at the home. She said that both she and Larry were home and if I wanted to come over, that was great. "Ok Catherine, she said she and her husband are home." "What are you going to say?" "I don't know, do you want to come." "I would love to." "Good, let's go."

We took off and headed to Deena's house. We talked about what I could say and how I could ask about Larry's father. We got off the freeway and Deena's house was just a few blocks away. I turned down the main street and I could not believe what I saw. "Catherine, Look to your right." Catherine turned to her right and there it was. The school, with a big banner in front "Christmas Pageant Tonight" I don't believe it, Anthony; your dream is coming true. That's a little scary, don't you think." "Catherine, I just had a feeling after the dream last night that this whole thing is starting to come to a conclusion." We got to Deena's house and I introduced Catherine. We walked in and sat down. Deena of course wanted to show off her baby and that gave me an opportunity to find out some information. "So Larry, are your parents excited at their grandchild?" My mom is, but I my dad passed away a week before I was born, so I never met him, but I still have his last name." "Oh my God, that's terrible. Did he have any extended family that you know?" "The only thing that I know is that he had a brother, but I never met him. I sure would love to meet him and show him his great Nephew." "That would be fantastic. What was your father's name?" "Dennis Crane" We thought of naming our baby after him, but when we both heard the wind blow and the sound it made was "Walter", we had to go with it." "Ok, when do you want me to start on your plans?" "Right away" Deena said with excitement. "We are real excited that you are back and are going to get us started." "Ok, Catherine and I are going to go, I will call you when my first draft is done." "Thank you Anthony, and very nice to meet you Catherine. If you want any dirt on Anthony, feel free to call me." "I think she will pass on that Deena," "Don't worry Anthony; I will hold some stuff back." "Catherine jumped in, "Deena, I noticed that they are having a Christmas Pageant across the street at the school." "Yea, Larry and I are going to take Walter to see it. Since it is his first Christmas, and it is so close it might be fun." "That does sound like fun, have a great time." With that Catherine and I left.

"Well, Catherine what do you think about that." "It all seems surreal, what are you going to do?" I am going to see Walter again and try to talk him into coming to the Christmas Pageant with me tonight." "What are you going to say that will convince him?" "I am going to try and convince him to come and see his

Nephew." "Are you sure that Larry is his brothers son." "No, but I now know his name is Dennis Crane and he died before his son was born, so that should be enough information for Walter to give me a shot." :When are you going to go?" As soon as I drop you off. The Show is at 7 PM and it is 4 PM now, so I don't have much time. I dropped off Catherine, and she wished me good luck, but then she did something strange. She hugged me and told me to be very careful; "Anthony, I have a very queasy feeling in my stomach, remember your dealing with more than just Deena, Larry and Walter. You're dealing with 2 spirits that have been following you for months, do you really think you know what they want?" "Catherine, I am confident that what they want is to get Walter back with his Nephew and Great Nephew." "Remember how at the beginning of all this, Jenny told me that her father was sad and lonely?" "Yes." "Well, if I can get him to meet his family tonight, then he won't be lonely anymore, he will have people who will love him, and that's what Jenny wants, I know it." "Is there any way I can stop you from going tonight." "Maybe if you let the night pass and the Christmas Pageant is over, then Jenny will go away and find some other way to get her father back with his family." "Catherine, I need to complete the circle that Jenny has created. Just think how she has manipulated this situation. She chose me and Deena and Larry and their baby. They have given me the information I need to convince Walter to come with me. Please Catherine, don't worry, this will be all over tonight." "Will you call me when it's over?" "Of course, In fact, why don't we have a late dinner and we can celebrate, Ok." "Ok" "Let me see you smile" "She gave me a smile and I gave her a kiss. She reluctantly let me out of her hug and then I left.

Two Thirty Four

I wake up every morning
As the alarm bells start to chime
But the hour never changes
Why is Two Thirty Four stuck in my mind

On my way over to Walters condo, I was thinking about how all this started and how Jenny was in the park and the dreams, I really feel like I am going to get Walter to come with me tonight, I don't know why, but I just have that feeling. I parked in front of Walters's condo and I walked up to the door. I knocked and Walter answered. "Hello Walter, do you remember me." "How could I forget, I had a hard time getting past your visit. Why are you here now, I told you I did not want to go back to the past, it's too hard and painful." "I understand, but I have some information for you that I think you should know." "What if I don't want to know, will you just go away and leave me alone." "I will go away, after you hear me out." "Let's sit."

"First, did you have a brother named Dennis?" "How did you know that?" "Ever since I left here, Jenny has not left me alone. I was working in Lake Tahoe for a month, but she continued to haunt me. I told you about the cologne, and I told you about the swing in my friend's house, the house that you owned. But this is where it gets even crazier." "My friend Deena, had a baby and her and her husband named the Baby "Walter". "Why did they name the baby "Walter" They both said they were sitting in the back yard and they heard the wind blowing through the tree's and it sounded like "Walter." So that's what they named their baby." "Ok, what does that have to do with me?" "Do you want to know what the baby's full name is?" "Sure." "Walter Crane." "What" "Walter, I believe that baby is your Brothers grandson and your Great Nephew." "Why do you think that?" "Deena's husband's name is "Larry Crane", His father, who died one week before he was born, was named "Dennis Crane." "I believe he was your brother." "This is too much, yes, my brother Died, but I never knew he had a son. I never even knew who he was with at the time." "That's Ok; this is your chance to meet your family." "I think this is what all this is about, Jenny and Laura have been hounding me for months and manipulating Deena and Larry's life in order to get you with your family." "It is so farfetched." "If I were in your shoes, I would feel the same way, but I know that Jenny wants you at the Christmas Pageant tonight, because Deena is going to bring her baby to the pageant." "I don't want to go to the Christmas Pageant that is a memory, I don't want to relive." "I think Jenny wants you there, because she was so happy that night before the accident, It's her last happy memory with you. That's what I believe she wants you to relive."

Walter sat there silent for a couple of minutes and then he said, "I will go with you." "Great, we better leave now, the Pageant starts at 7 PM. We left for the pageant and the drive was a very quiet one. I know he's scared and confused, but I hope that after tonight, he will be a little happier then he has been for the last several years. I know meeting his family will not take away the pain of what he lost, but at least he will have family to be with and that should give him some relief, at least that's what I hope.

We arrived at the school with about 5 minutes to spare. I could see in Walters face that he was feeling very apprehensive about this and I have to give him a lot of credit for coming with me. If I were in his shoes, I doubt if I would have come, in fact I probably would have called the police on me. We parked and headed inside. I asked Walter if he was Ok, and he said he was. We entered the building and it was packed. I looked for Deena, and I saw her sitting a few rows from the back. I showed Walter where they were and he could see Larry and his namesake Walter. I could feel my phone vibrate in my pocket, but I could not answer, so I let it go voice mail. I looked at the message and it was Catherine. The message read *"Anthony, you need to call me right away, I found the answer to the 234 and it's not the time, it's a song. Please call me!"*

That did not seem that important, so I will call her when we leave here. I told Walter that we should wait until the pageant is over and then I will introduce him. We sat through the songs and looking at Walter, I know this is bringing up those hard memories of the night 45 years ago that his family were taken from him. I also wonder if Jenny is here and if she is finally satisfied that I have done what she wanted. The pageant was coming to an end and I told Walter that I would go over and talk to Deena. As people were starting to leave the room, I made my way to Deena.

"Hello Deena." "Anthony, what are you doing here?" "I have to talk to you and Larry for a minute; I want to introduce you to someone." "Ok" "Deena, Why don't we sit down over where the people have gone so we can have some privacy." "It sounds serious." "It is, in a good way." We walked to the corner of the room and I called Walter over. "Deena, Larry, This is Walter." "Hello Walter, nice to meet you," Then Deena said, "My baby is named Walter, what a coincidence." "Deena, Larry, I'm going to explain something to you and you may have a hard time believing it, so please allow me a little time to explain, even if it sounds too hard to believe, Ok." "Anthony, we have know each other a long time, when you sound this serious, I will listen." "Ok, Here goes, Larry, Hold on to your seat, Walter is your uncle." "My uncle!" "Yes, your father is Walters Brother." "How do you know that?" "Well it gets a little complicated, but when your father died, the two brothers were not close, so he had no Idea who his Brother was with or that she was pregnant." "I still don't understand." "Deena, you called me after not seeing me in a couple of years, and that was not just out of the blue, now this is where you are going to have to hang in with me, because it is going to get weird."" Anthony," Deena jumped in, " I think we are past weird" "Walter Crane, 45 years ago owned the home you live in now, I found that out by looking up the tax records." Larry still very confused" "Why would you look up the tax records?" "Walter's family was killed 45 years ago after they attended a Christmas Pageant just like this one. They were killed by crossing the street right in front of the school, by a car." "After that, Walter sold the home and moved, but his daughter, Jenny for some reason has picked me to bring him back to meet his extended family, meaning you." "Your right Anthony, In all the years I have know you, this is the strangest thing you have ever said." "I know, but you will understand."

" I could not sleep one night, so I took a walk in the park. It was 3 AM and I saw a little girl playing on a swing. She ran when she saw me, but the next night she was there again. We talked that night and she told me about her father and how he was lonely and sad. For the next several months, even in Tahoe, she became part of my dreams." Larry was sitting and listening, but in disbelief, and Deena said, "It still sounds crazy." "I know, but one dream was so real, I even met her mother, Walters's wife, in the dream and both of them, wanted my help to get Walter to come here." "Anthony, I never thought of you as a believer in ghosts""I never was, but things change. The first time I met with Walter, he refused to come with me, because the memory of the night his family was killed was too much for him and he did not want to re live." Deena reached out and grabbed Walter hand. "I'm so sorry Walter." "What had me look up the tax records was when you told me that you named your baby Walter, because you heard the name in the wind. I knew Jenny was manipulating me and I now wondered if she manipulated you two, in order to get you to name your baby "Walter, so I had a feeling and I looked up the tax records. When I found out that Walter had owned the home, I knew that this was some kind of twisted situation. You met Catherine today, When I told her, about the dreams and everything that has been happening with me and Jenny, she started helping me research, and we found everything about what happened 45 years ago. The last two dreams I had, gave me the ability to go back to Walter and convince him to come with me today." Larry finally asked a question. "Anthony, I don't know you very well, but What your telling us makes no sense. Do you really want us to believe that the ghost of a little girl somehow told us to name our baby Walter?"

"Larry, Believe me, I understand your skepticism, but you will understand, I promise." "Ok, please go on." "First I was in Tahoe and I had a dream that Walters's wife, Laura came to me and told me that Walter had lost a brother. Last night, I had a dream about this Pageant and Both of you were here with me and Walter was also here and you also had your baby. When I called you this morning, I was telling Catherine about the dreams and I realized I needed to know about Larry's father, because I thought he could be Walters's brother."

"Larry, When you told me the circumstances of your father's death and you told me his name, that gave me the information I needed to go back to Walter and try and talk him into coming with me tonight. When I told him your father's name was Dennis, that convinced him." "That's amazing, but I am still not convinced that my father is Walters's brother." Deena, remember when you told me about the little girl that visited you after you had the baby." "Yes, she was a very nice little girl with beautiful Blue/Green eyes." Deena, that was Walters daughter, Jenny" "You're kidding me." "I wish I was." "Larry, did you ever see a picture of your father?" "Yes, my mom had many pictures." "Well. Walter is going to show you a picture of himself and your father, of course it was many years ago." Walter took the picture out of his wallet and showed it to Larry and Deena. The look on Larry's face was of acceptance and he started to tear up. He stood up and gave Walter a hug. "Walter, there is so much I want to talk to you about." "Will you tell me about my father?" "I would love to Larry." Deena, then stood up and Handed Walter her son, "Walter, meet your name sake." Walter, with tears in his eyes, took the little baby in his arms and held him with such gentleness and love, I even started to well up. Then Deena said, "Anthony, the story is amazing, but where did I fit in?" "Well Deena, let's just say that your marriage was defiantly made in heaven." "I think I understand."

Larry invited us to the house, so we all started to walk over; it was just a couple of blocks away. As we got outside the school, there was a man near the street preaching and holding up a sign that said "Save your Soul" He was a tall man with long stringy hair and a beard. His clothes were old and he looked as though he was homeless. I did not want him bothering Walter or his new family, so I put myself between them and he came over to me and handed me a prayer card. I took it, thanked him and put it in my back pocket and we continued on our way. I thought that may have been Jenny's way of contacting me, but I don't know. We got to their home and the reunion began. Larry wanted Walter to stay, so they could talk and he said that he would take Walter home. They thanked me and I told them I would be in contact with the plans and I Left. As I was walking back to my truck, I felt really good. I believe now with all my heart that I did what Jenny and Laura wanted. I brought Walter to them and he is not lonely anymore. He has some people who will love him and I believe now that that's what Jenny wanted all along. Why she picked me, I have no idea and probably will never know.

As I was crossing the street I realized that I did not call Catherine back. Her voicemail said the 234 was a song, so now I'm interested. I took the phone out of my pocket and as soon as I started to dial Headlights blinded me and I heard the screeching of the tires. Before I knew it I was flying through the air. It was just like the dream I had, only this time I was feeling a lot of pain. As I landed on the ground. I started to roll and I could feel my flesh tearing away from my body. My head was bouncing off the pavement and when I finally came to a stop, I was battered. I did not know what to do, there was no one around and I could not get up. I wanted to pray, but I could not think. Then I remembered the religious guy who handed me the prayer card. I reached to my pocket and tried to get the card. I could barely move, but I was able to grab the card with two fingers. The pain was extraordinary. I brought the card to my face, but the blood was covering my eyes. I wiped the blood and put the card close. When I saw what it said I could not believe it. Now I know what Catherine was calling about, but the voice mail to text transcribed it wrong. 234 wasn't a song. It was Psalm 23:4

Yea, though I walk through the valley of the shadow of death, I will fear no evil: for thou art with me; thy rod and thy staff they comfort me.

Catherine was right all along, the 234 was the key. Jenny said she would know before I did. I guess I should have listened to Catherine when she said she had a very bad feeling. I just put my head on the ground and felt so cold and alone.

Then, I felt someone take my hand. I again wiped the blood away from my eyes to see who was there. My eyes were blurry, but I could see that it was Jenny. "Get up Anthony, we have to go." "Jenny, I'm really hurt, can't you see, there is blood everywhere." "Jenny leaned over and her green eyes were large and bright and as I looked into them, I could see my reflection. There was no blood, no scratches; in fact I looked like nothing had happened at all. "Let's go Anthony." I got up and I said, "Jenny, where are we going." "Were going home" I looked past her and the path ahead was lit so bright and then I remembered what Jenny had told me on Halloween. She asked me what I saw when I looked at her and I said that I saw a very sweet little girl, but she said "No, you see the light that will light the way" Now I understand, she is lighting the way and maybe that's why I was picked by her. She was to light my way, but before she did, she needed me to give her father a new life. I guess for me, the last 8 months were just a road to get where I'm going and the little girl on the swing in the Wee Hours of the Morning is going to lead the way.

Anthony D Cantelmo

Made in the USA
Las Vegas, NV
24 December 2021

39327511R00080